Project Bloodborn

Book 3
Wolf Killer

Craig Zerf

Anglo American Press

LONDON, UNITED KINGDOM

Once again –

For my wife, Polly and my

son, Axel

Your light chases the

shadows from my soul.

The tiger and the lion may be more powerful – but the Wolf does not perform in the circus.
Anonymous

I thought I was the only one who had that satellite number,' said Brenner, keeping his eyes on the road as he drove.

'Almost,' admitted Griff as he cut the connection. 'Only one other person has it. Sandra.'

'Your sister?'

'The one and only.'

'I never met her,' noted Brenner.

'Yes, you did. We flew back after that one Christmas, nineteen sixty-seven. The battle of *Ong Thanh*. Remember, you got shot in the leg and I had some R&R coming so we took the freedom bird home for two weeks. You met her then.'

Brenner shook his head. 'I remember the battle, not the sister. Anyway, she sounded stressed. What gives?'

'It's my niece, Tiffany, she's gone AWOL again.'

'This happen much?'

'Yep, she's sixteen now, going on thirty-five. Real nightmare. Normally they wait a few days and she comes home again. But this time she's hooked up with a real bad crowd.'

'Drugs?'

'Worse, apparently. Devil worshippers.'

Brenner snorted. 'What? You mean like naked dancing around a fire and sacrificing goats? It's all bullshit, man. She'll get bored and go home as soon as the novelty wears off.'

'What if the whole thing turns into a Charles Manson thing, and she ends up murdering some celebrity?'

'Manson wasn't a devil worshiper,' argued Brenner. 'Just a dick with a swastika tattooed on his forehead.'

'Well, what about those two teenagers who shot up that school in Columbine? They were devil worshippers.'

Brenner shook his head. 'Goths. Not the same thing at all.'

Griff frowned.

'Hey, dude,' said Brenner. 'If you're concerned then let's go take a look around. I mean, it's not as if we got some big corporate deadline to stick to. We're free agents, man. Where are they?'

'They live in Carbonate, Arizona. It's a little town outside of where Frisco used to be back in the day. A group of around three hundred people who reprocess the old silver mines left over from the silver and gold rush era of the mid eighteen hundreds. Fact is, there's about three or four little communities around that area that do the same. It truly is in the middle of nowhere, but they got a school and facilities. Water, lights.'

Brenner consulted the map in his head. 'It's about a fourteen-hour drive. We can stop halfway, or whenever we see an appropriate spot.'

Griff smiled. 'Thanks.'

'Sure thing,' responded Brenner.

The blacktop unrolled underneath them as the Winnebago ate up the miles. They stopped to gas up once, then stopped a second time a few miles past Lordsburg, New Mexico, pulling off the road and driving a mile or two down a barely discernible track to park up in amongst a pile of boulders and scrub.

They decamped early the next morning and Griff drove the last few hours. They hit the little town of Kingman, Arizona at around nine in the morning, driving through the center. It was big enough to boast a Walmart and an In-N-Out Burger.

Griff pulled up at the drive through to the In-N-Out. 'What you want?' he asked Brenner.

'Get me two double quarter pounders with cheese.'

'This isn't McDonalds. They don't have quarter pounders.'

'What they got?'

Griff peered at the menu. 'Something called a Quad-Quad. Same thing, I think.'

'Okay then. Two of those and a large soda.'

Griff ordered the same for himself and moments later they were on the road again, heading some thirty more miles west of Kingman. Brenner ate Griff's second Quad-Quad burger. The old man didn't complain. One had been sufficient for him.

The land was inhospitable, but at the same time beautiful in its savagery. Rose colored sand, massive rocks and boulders interspersed with scrub and stunted trees. After a while, the road petered out, losing the blacktop to graded dirt and eventually to rough track.

The town of Carbonate was less a town and more of a semi-permanent campsite. Both single and double-wide trailer homes. Some timber-framed commercial buildings. A main street that looked like a façade from a nineteen fifties movie set. A squat water tower with the town name painted on it.

The main street had been blacktopped at some stage, but time and weather had taken its toll and only patches remained. Like blackened scabs in the dirt.

A barber, bakery, general goods store with a gas pump outside, a dressmaker, beauty salon, hardware store, funeral parlor, doctor's rooms, a saloon with what appeared to be rooms above it. Also, a gun shop, one of the largest establishments in the micro-town.

But the whole area was clean, graffiti free and the stores looked well stocked.

Griff drove through the town and turned left at the first road, following his sister's directions. They pulled up outside a blue double-wide. Above ground pool, mangy lawn, picket fence, and a well maintained, but dusty, 1996 Ford Bronco that used to be red but was now a sun-faded salmon-pink.

As they climbed out of the Winnebago, two massive pit bulls came racing around the side of the trailer, mouths open and teeth bared. They took one look at Brenner and rolled over onto their backs with such alacrity it looked as though they had been shot.

Brenner clicked his fingers and the pair of dogs stood and slunk over to him, heads hanging submissively, ears flat. He leaned down and patted them, causing them to wag their tails so hard their bodies bounced up and down on the spot.

The door opened, and a late middle-aged woman walked out. She was of average height, home-dyed blonde hair, knee length sleeveless green dress that exposed well sculpted arms and legs, tight from manual labor as opposed to hours spent in an air-conditioned gym.

'I'm sorry about the dogs,' she said in way of greeting. 'They broke through the back gate.' Then she ran forward and threw her arms around Griff. 'Hey, big bro. You came.'

'Of course,' said Griff. 'Why wouldn't I? You're my favorite sister.'

'I'm your only sister.'

Griff nodded. 'There is that, but even if you weren't, you'd still be my fave. This is Brenner. I'm sure you've met before, but he says not. Brenner, this is Sandra, my sis.'

Sandra held out her hand and Brenner shook it. Her grasp was firm, hand dry and she looked him in the eyes when she shook. He liked her straight away.

She shook her head. 'We haven't met,' she said.

'Yeah, you have,' insisted Griff. 'Back in sixty-eight. Maybe sixty-nine.'

Sandra looked at the man with the twenty-five-year-old face standing opposite her and laughed. 'What, when I was ten and he wasn't even born? I hope you aren't going senile, old bro.'

Griff frowned then joined in with her laughter. 'Of course, must have been thinking of someone else. Obviously. So, how's Joe?'

'He's inside. Come on, let's get you guys something to eat and drink.'

They followed Sandra, the dogs walking so close to Brenner as to keep getting tangled in his legs.

Sandra led them through to the sitting room. A man stood to greet them. He hugged Griff, slapping him on the back as he did so then he extended his hand to Brenner. They shook.

'Name's Joe.'

'Brenner. Pleased to meet you.'

Sandra opened a few beers and handed them around. There was no offer of glasses, it wasn't that sort of house.

Brenner openly appraised Joe. He seemed a quiet man, confident, slow-moving but not slow-witted. And after a quick glance at his eyes, Brenner knew. 'So, Joe,' he asked. 'Where did you serve?'

'Afghanistan. Marines. And you?'

Brenner shrugged. 'Overseas. Here and there.'

Joe nodded. 'Spec ops.'

It was a statement, not a question so Brenner didn't reply.

'So, talk to me,' said Griff. 'Where is my wayward niece? What trouble has she got herself into this time?'

Joe sighed. 'We know where she is. Look, I could just cruise in there, try to strong-arm the bunch of them and bring her home. But even if that worked, she would just go again. We were hoping you could convince her to leave the group she's with, Griff. You've always been the only one she listens to.'

'Why can't you play the waiting game?' asked Brenner. 'You know, leave her for a while, keep an eye on the situation and wait for it to fizzle out. Then she'll come home on her own accord.'

Sandra shook her head. 'Normally, that's the way we play it,' she admitted. 'But this time, it's different. I've met some of the kids she's shacked up with. They're all around eighteen to mid-twenties, and there's something wrong about them. I'm not talking Goth wanabees,' continued Sandra. 'I'm talking proper scary here.'

'What are we talking,' asked Griff. 'Weapons, violence, that sort of thing?'

Both Joe and Sandra shook their heads again. 'No,' said Joe. 'It's like Sandra told you on the phone. I know this sounds weird but we're talking evil. Devil worshipping. Old Testament stuff. Feelings of dread and darkness. Animal sacrifice, weird ceremonies. People have watched from a distance. It's not just us. Other families have been affected.'

Joe took a deep breath and scrubbed his eyes with the back of his hands. Brenner noticed for the first time how exhausted the two parents were. And something else. More than exhaustion. Fear. They were both terrified and they were doing their very best to cover the fact with a veneer of normality. A thin armor of domesticity. Beer and sandwiches and Sunday football.

It wasn't working.

'I've seen shit, man,' continued Joe. 'In Afghanistan. Death, torture. Raving fanatics willing to die for their own twisted cause. Seen friends die. Killed men. But when I went to get Tiffany back from the house she's sharing with these dudes … it was different. I was scared, man. Really scared. There was this dude, twenty something. Dead eyes. Told me to walk away, and I did. Had to before I lost it completely. Took all my willpower not to piss my pants and run, screaming.'

'Did you see Tiffany?' asked Griff.

'Yeah. She was there. Looked happy. Had a stupid grin on her face. Like she was idolizing the main dude. Like a look of reverence.'

Sandra drew a deep breath and started crying, softly. 'Over the last few weeks, the surrounding towns have lost over twenty young adults to this crowd. And more go every day. Tiffany is the only one under eighteen. We phoned the sheriff's department, but they said there's nothing much they can do. They could bring her back, but they wouldn't be able to stop her leaving again. And as she was there of her own free will, they would find it difficult to press any charges. Obviously, we couldn't mention the whole devil worshipping thing. How could we?'

Griff nodded. 'Fine. This evening, Brenner and I will go take a recce of this place. We'll formulate a plan based on what we see. But let me assure you, this ends today. When the sun rises tomorrow it will be on a fresh new day, a day without any of these problems. I guarantee this.'

'As do I,' added Brenner.

Sandra burst into tears.

CHAPTER TWO

Sergeant Solomon Hopewell shook his head and tutted under his breath as he stared at the shattered remains of what used to be a sturdy front door.

'Lenny,' he said. 'You are going to have to learn some sort of control, or what use are you to me? Seriously, old chap, if you can't even open a door without bashing it to smithereens, then it really does narrow down your usefulness to that of simply smashing things up. And that's hardly much of a skill set, is it?'

Lenny looked at the ground. Ashamed. 'Sorry, mister Solomon.'

'It's sergeant, Lenny. Sergeant Solomon. Oh well, let's take a look around and see what we can deduct from the scene of the crime, as it were.'

Solomon ghosted about the house, sniffing at patches of blood, staring intently at the broken doors and brushing aside the forest of yellow police tape.

'Six guards,' he muttered. 'All died fast. The main target died here, the doctor. And he died hard. Loads of blood. He was being punished.' He nodded to himself. 'This was Brenner. Definitely. And the man who died hard, well, we must assume that once again the Wolfman is on some sort of moral crusade. Right, Lenny, let's all go to the ranch our informant told us about and see if we can get a good lead on our friendly neighborhood werewolf. Because the one thing about Brenner, is he leaves a wide trail.'

CHAPTER THREE

The barn was surrounded by six trailers. All in need of repair. Piles of trash dotted the area around the rusting dwellings. Beer cans, empty cereal boxes, milk cartons.

There were no dogs. In fact, the entire area seemed devoid of wildlife in any shape or size. No birds and no bees.

The remnants of a large bonfire lay smoking outside the entrance to the barn, broken chairs, three-legged stools and upturned crates circled the fire. The cultists version of a sitting room.

All the people were presently inside the ramshackle barn. Both Griff and Brenner could plainly hear them chanting. A single male voice leading then the congregation taking up the cadence.

'What's he saying?' asked Griff, knowing Brenner's supernatural hearing would pick up the voices like they were next to him.

Brenner shrugged. 'It's not English. Not sure it's even real words. Not Latin as far as I can tell. But it has a rhythm and a structure.'

'Let's move closer,' said Griff.

The two of them crawled forward, confident they wouldn't be seen. They had waited until nightfall to recon the place, trusting the darkness would conceal them until they deemed it necessary to be seen.

Also, Brenner liked the dark. The dark was his friend.

They moved to within a few feet of the ring of trailers.

Griff carried a weapon. A Colt .45, upgraded to a Para Ordnance version, turning the seven-shot weapon into a high capacity fourteen-shot.

Brenner was a weapon. Upgraded from normal humanity to a weapon of mass destruction.

As they got closer the droning invocation from the group of worshipers grew louder, and Griff started to slow down until, after a minute or so, he had stopped moving forward completely.

'What's up?' asked Brenner.

Griff shook his head and Brenner could see his friend was sweating and shaking, his face a deathly pallor. 'I can't go on,' he whispered.

'Why? You hurt?'

Again, Griff shook his head. 'My body just refuses to move. It's that chant. Whatever it is.' He looked at Brenner, his eyes wide with surprise. 'I'm fucking terrified, man,' he admitted. 'I don't think I've ever been so shit-scared in my entire life. And that includes Cambodia. This place is evil, Ded. Let's get out of here. Please.'

Brenner grabbed Griff's arm and crawled backwards, dragging the old man with him. After they had backed off around fifty feet, Griff seemed to come to his senses.

'I'm alright,' he grunted. 'Don't know what that was, but I sure as hell don't want to feel that again.' He looked at Brenner. 'You didn't feel anything?'

The big man shook his head. 'No. Nothing. Sorry. Look, you stay here, I'll cruise back for a closer look.

Stay put, dude, there's obviously something amiss here.'

Griff laid his hand on Brenner's shoulder. 'Careful, Ded,' he said. 'There's power there. Watch yourself.'

Brenner grinned. 'I'll be fine, trust me.'

He crawled into the night, moving faster than a running man, now he was unencumbered by company.

***

Damballa Gorgon, the grand high prince of Lucifer and head of the newly formed 'Church of Lust', adjusted his goat mask and continued to pray. His actual name was, or had been, Miles Bartley. He was twenty-four years old, attractive and slightly above average intelligence.

If you asked him to describe himself, he would tell you he was outgoing, popular, although he didn't have as many close friends as he might due to people's envy and jealousy. He was goal oriented and emotionally stable, never suffering from anxiety or feelings of remorse or inadequacy. Charming and generous to a fault, and humbly aware he was vastly superior to all those around him.

He saw himself as adored, respected, and revered.

If asked to sum himself up in one word he would have chosen - leader.

Any clinical psychologist would have summed his personality up in a different word - sociopath.

But he was a true believer in the Morningstar. Lucifer. The father of all lies. And like any true believe he took it upon himself to testify. To preach and to spread the word.

And the message was - do as you will.

Damballa had grown up in the town of Grand Strike, some twelve miles from Carbonate. Like Carbonate, Grand Strike was a re-mining community, using modern methods to rework the mines that had been so profitable back in the 1800's.

They say the Devil finds work for idle hands, and this had definitely been the case with Miles, or Damballa as he liked to be known now. Like all those before him he had three choices when he had finished schooling. Leave, work the mines, or work in one of the few shops in the area.

He had exercised a fourth option. He stayed, but simply lived at his parents' home and done nothing. At first his parents had attempted to force him to find a job, but they soon learned that although Miles could be charming if he wanted, he could also be frighteningly cruel and harsh to those who got on his wrong side.

Those who erred found that bad things happened to them. Family pets would disappear. Motor vehicles would suffer brake failure, and household water supplies would become contaminated with raw sewage or worse. Nothing that could be pinned on Miles, but everyone knew.

So, they ignored him as much as possible, allowing a cancer of evil to grow unabated in their midst.

Then, one day, they simply left. No forwarding address, no goodbyes. They were there, then they weren't. Suspicions were expressed, and fingers pointed, but there seemed to be no proof of foul play, so Miles was left to stew in his own fetid juices.

It was at this time he turned to the internet for guidance. Studying the works of Anton LaVey, the father of Satanism. However, he found the teachings of LaVey to be far too liberal and weak, so he delved deeper into the darkness. Animal sacrifice, forbidden rites, and dark rituals.

Over time, Miles became Damballa, a true practitioner of the dark arts. And just as there is much visible goodness in the world, there is also its counterbalance. True evil. And with that evil, comes power.

The power to control, the power to hurt, and the power to command.

Damballa collected to him all the youths who felt rudderless. Those who despised the small towns in which they lived, those who saw no point to their mundane existences, and those who merely wanted to belong.

There were over thirty of them now, controlled by himself and his two lieutenants of darkness.

The congregation chanted along with Damballa, swaying from side to side as they did so. Letting the power of their master wash over them.

Around the black alter in front of them burned six black candles. And on the alter itself, lay the life ready for sacrifice. A black Labrador. Its legs had been trussed up and a length of duct tape had been wound around its muzzle to stop it barking.

The dog gazed at the crowd with sad eyes. Fearful, but trusting in its master. Knowing that the man would allow no harm to come to his best friend.

Damballa raised the sacrificial knife above his head as the chanting reached a crescendo.

And the dog whined and wagged its tail as the dark priest approached.

CHAPTER FOUR

Brenner peeked into the barn via the large double doors that had been left ajar. Thirty plus people were gathered around a central character. They were all dressed in rough cassocks, like amateur-dramatic versions of Friar Tuck. Their heads bare, faces shining with a mixture of adulation and respect.

Except for the head honcho who was dressed in a red velvet gown, and on his head a mask of a goat. The mask was obviously home-embellished, real goat skin stretched over a store-bought Halloween mask. Two small horns added afterward.

But the very incompetent crudity of the disguise had its own chilling effect. The torn skin, the rough stitching, the obvious joins where the horns stuck out. The misshapen eye holes.

Then Brenner saw the dog lying helpless on the alter. The knife held above it. He kicked the doors open and strode in.

'Stop,' he shouted. 'You hurt the dog, I hurt you. Understand?'

As one, the congregation turned to look at the intruder.

The man in the velvet gown pointed at him and screamed. 'How dare you crash into our church uninvited? This is a private ceremony. Leave now and

I may allow you to live. Stay, and you shall feel the wrath of the dark lord.'

'Shut it, goat boy,' stated Brenner as he pushed his way through the crowd and stopped in front of the dog. Using his bare hands, he grabbed the rope they had used to truss the hound up and simply snapped it. Then, working with great care, he gently pulled the duct tape from the dog's muzzle. As soon as he had finished, the Labrador licked his face then rolled over onto its back in full submission.

'He has defiled the ritual,' screeched Damballa. 'He must be punished.'

Brenner took a step forward and ripped the goat mask off the screaming man's face. What he saw surprised him. An average young man, orderly features, clean shaven, and well groomed. But with eyes that positively radiated power. And insanity. Industrial quantities of both.

Spittle formed around goat boys' lips as he flew into a rage and grabbed for the mask, shouting obscenities as he did so.

'He has insulted the master,' yelled one of the lieutenants. 'He must be punished.'

The crowd surged forward. Many of them had drawn weapons. Long bladed knives and machetes. One young man even had a broadsword, a cheap Chinese made knockoff suited more to cosplay than actual warfare.

With a growl, Brenner exploded into Wolfman form, shredding his clothes and boots, growing to over seven feet and four hundred pounds. Canines like daggers, and claws like scythes glinted in the candlelight as he threw back his head and howled.

There was approximately two seconds of absolute silence then the entire congregation ran screaming to the exit.

All except for Damballa and his two lieutenants. They stood firm. Damballa because he was an insane believer, and his lieutenants because, almost unbelievably, they were more scared of Damballa than they were of the Wolfman.

Damballa threw his arms wide and declaimed. 'Oh, Amon and Balam. Oh, great Phenex, thanks be to our Lord and principal who has sent this demon to serve us.'

'You think I'm here to serve you, boy?' growled Brenner.

'Silence,' commanded Damballa. 'You shall speak only when given permission from your betters.'

Brenner shook his head then casually backhanded the self-styled priest of darkness. The blow lifted the goat boy off his feet and slammed him into the alter, sending the dog scurrying for cover.

Damballa shook his head in disbelief that his minion had dared harm him. Then, in a moment of epiphany, reality caught up with his self-absorbed perception and he saw before him what was really there. What was truly standing in front of him.

His face collapsed as the truth revealed itself. He started to shake in both fury and fear. 'Wings,' he whispered to himself. 'He has wings.'

Next to him, his two lieutenants fell to their knees.

'You sully this temple with your presence,' screamed Damballa, his outrage overcoming his fear. 'Defiler.' Pulling a blade from beneath his gown he launched himself at Brennerwolf, striking down hard as he did so.

But it was to no avail. Even with his fanatic-enhanced speed and strength he was like an insect trapped in amber. The Wolfman struck him down with great vengeance and righteous anger. His bisected torso fell to the floor, pumping out its life's blood as it did so.

Both the lieutenants averted their eyes and bowed their heads in acquiescence as the dark angel in front of them destroyed their master, utterly and completely. The candles all guttered and flickered out. The doors burst open, and a clean wind scoured through the building, driving out the smell of incense and blood and unwashed humanity.

And the Wolfman threw his head back and howled.

CHAPTER FIVE

Brenner took a drag of his cigarette as he leaned down and scratched the dogs behind their ears. Their tongues lolled out the sides of their mouths as they wriggled with pleasure.

He didn't need to turn to know Griff had walked up behind him.

'She's okay,' said the old man. 'Can't seem to remember a lot of what happened. Like she was in a thrall. She remembers you, though. She remembers the Wolfman. As do most of the kids that were there.'

'What about the body?' asked Brenner.

'Taken care of. This is a mining community. The remains are already buried so far underground it would need an archeological dig to find them. They take care of their own here. As it should be. They're all very thankful for what you did.'

Brenner took another drag. 'I sense a "but" coming on.'

Griff nodded. 'But, they would like us to leave. The whole Wolfman thing has made them very uncomfortable. Even though most of them don't actually believe it. They think the kids suffered some sort of mass hysterical illusion. Anyway, they all agreed it would be better for the kids if we went. Allow them to recover. Maybe give them some sort of safe space, or some new age crap like that.'

'Kids?'

'What's that?' asked Griff.

'You keep saying kids. How old would you say their average age is?'

Griff shrugged. 'Don't know. Eighteen, maybe nineteen.'

'When we were in 'Nam, the average age of the combat soldier was nineteen,' stated Brenner. 'We didn't get no safe space. Instead, we got shot at. Killed. We learned about the monsters that lived in the dark.' The big man ground out the cigarette stub under his boot. 'Fucking safe space.'

'Yeah,' agreed Griff. 'It's all bullshit. Come on, let's go.'

Brenner didn't say anything, instead he headed for the back door, opened it and went inside.

'Hey,' called Griff. 'Not a good idea, man. I think we should just leave.'

'We will leave,' said Brenner. 'After we've had a talk.'

He walked into the sitting room. The small room was full of people. Four teenagers and six adults including Joe, Sandra, and Tiffany. He also recognized one of the lieutenants.

Everyone stopped talking as he entered the room and the teenagers visibly flinched and pulled away.

Brenner looked at Joe. 'So,' he said. 'You have your daughter back.'

Joe nodded and mumbled a thank you.

'You reckon you can keep her this time?' asked the big man.

No one answered.

Finally, an older man stood and addressed Brenner. 'Thank you for helping us with our problem,' he said. 'I think you'll find we can take it from here. Given a bit of time and caring, the kids will be fine. Don't feel you have to stay on our behalf.'

There was a murmur of agreement from the rest of the adults.

Brenner shook his head. 'Those young men and women you call kids,' he said. 'They all drew down on me. Knives, machetes. Even a fucking sword. They were going to kill me. Or at least cut me up real bad.'

'I'm sure you're mistaken,' blustered the older man. 'Charlie would never do that.' He gestured toward the one Brenner recognized as a lieutenant.

Brenner raised an eyebrow. 'He was one of the leaders,' he said.

Again, no one spoke.

'Listen,' continued the big man. 'I'm not trying to cause unnecessary trouble. I just want you to realize this won't simply go away overnight. There was true evil here. Your sons and daughters were intimately involved in it. I have cut off the head, but who knows what may spring up next. They have done wrong and should be punished, not given safe places, or cuddly toys. They are adults who need to take responsibility. And until you all realize that, then your troubles will continue, in some form or other, until it all ends badly. You need to man-up. All of you.'

Without another word, Brenner walked out, followed by Griff who didn't even bother to say any goodbyes.

They climbed into the Winnebago and left, travelling west toward the heart of Arizona.

After ten minutes of silence Brenner said. 'You know something, Griff. I'm sick of helping people who act like I've just pissed in their porridge afterward. We pull their so-called kids out of the shit and they act like it was all our fault to begin with.'

Griff smiled. 'It's nothing personal, big man,' he said. 'It's just that people don't like to face their own failures. Take Joe. He's a good man. A strong man. He served his country. He's no coward. But he was unmanned by that devil-priest dude, and that shamed him. Then you went in there and sorted it all like it was no problem. I know he should have been thankful, and I'm sure he was, but every second he looked at you, he saw his own failure. His own perceived cowardice. His own fear and timidity. The same with them all. So, the sooner they could get rid of you, the sooner they can all go back to seeing themselves as they wish to.'

Neither of the two friends spoke for a while as the blacktop peeled away underneath them and the beautiful, barren landscape unrolled on either side like a movie backdrop.

Then Brenner said. 'It's a full moon tonight.'

CHAPTER SIX

Brandon Taylor played the part of the 'Good Ole Boy' to perfection. From the Southern homilies, to the string tie, gold belt buckle, and white Stetson, he oozed charisma, good manners, and a charming simplicity of thought. One of his favorite expressions was, 'I like to name names and call a spade a spade'.

And behind that bluff and homely exterior was the mind of a Machiavellian manipulator. A man unheard of outside of the industry, he was, to all intents and purposes, the power behind the throne of Exxon Oil. A company with an annual revenue in excess of four hundred billion dollars.

He stood at the head of the huge boardroom table and opened his arms wide, encompassing the three other men in the room.

The Russian from Gazprom, Oleg Barinov.

Lin Yang from PetroChina. And Fadil Ali, the Saudi Arabian from Aramco. It had been decided from the beginning all the big four would be represented, showing a united front against fossil energy's newest threat.

Brandon Taylor had disagreed, as had his head of security, Tony Valachi, who considered anyone who didn't openly support the NRA to be a pinko-liberal fag-loving traitor. And working with commies, ragheads, and dinks made him sick to the stomach. But he was a good soldier and did as he was told. He was currently in the adjoining room, listening to every word.

'Gentlemen,' said Taylor. 'The package has been secured.'

There was a polite smattering of applause.

'The target is currently being held in a safe house in a remote location and is guarded by a crack team made up of two members from each of our respective countries. Gentlemen, I would like to congratulate all involved and say that what we have achieved, true international cooperation, is something the politicians couldn't accomplish given a million years and a billion dollars.'

More applause. Some laughter.

'I will personally contact the principle,' continued Taylor. 'And make sure our demands are met. And now, gentlemen, please feel free to take some downtime. I urge you to see our fair city and, if possible, some of the magnificent state of Texas. The river walk is stupendous, and you should look at the Alamo. I mean, there's a shithouse full of stuff to see in this huge state of ours. And always remember, do you know why Texas is so big? Because we wanted it to be.'

Taylor slapped his thighs and laughed out loud.

This time, there was no applause.

CHAPTER SEVEN

The four-hundred-pound wolf ran hard, its body flying over the rose-colored sand and scattered rocks like it was an ethereal being. A spirit, as opposed to flesh and blood. Reveling in its freedom. It's strength. It's supernatural abilities.

Above it, the almost full moon bleached the landscape to a blue-white daguerreotype.

The night before, they had found a large finger of rock that pointed to the sky. It had been perfect to chain Brenner to, imprisoning the monster he became on the first night of every moon.

The next day both Griff and Brenner had decided to stay on in the wastelands, eschewing company for a while. Seeking the solitude of the land. Allowing the desert air to wash them clean of civilization.

Then the wolf abruptly stopped running, dropping to its belly. Frozen. Ears pricked up. Nostrils testing the midnight air.

Not moving.

The wind direction shifted slightly and there it was again. The unmistakable smell of gun oil. But not commercially available gun oil. It wasn't something a hunter or farmer might use on his rifle or shotgun. This was a more astringent smell. Deeper. It was RFG grease. Rapid Fire Gun grease for automatic weapons.

Over a mile away. Maybe even two or three. But it was there. The Wolfman's supernatural sense of smell was never wrong.

He lifted his head, took a deep breath then started to run in the direction of the scent. Keeping low, using the folds on the land to obscure. Moving swiftly but carefully.

A mile and a half. He stopped. Sniffed. Moved again.

A small ravine ahead. On his left, he could sense a presence. Inch by inch the wolf crept forward. His nose told him there were two men. Unwashed. No aftershave. No smell of cigarette smoke or soap. Professionals. Well hidden.

The wolf moved closer. A foxhole near the lip of the ravine. Tarpaulin covered with sand and scrubs. Perfectly camouflaged. But not to Brenner's night vision.

Two men, both of obvious Chinese extraction. They wore dark civilian clothes, black cargo pants, black T-shirts. Lightweight webbing. Both carried the type-85 silenced submachine gun. Chinese Special Forces issue.

Curious, thought Brenner. *That's something you don't see often.*

He wondered what they could be guarding so, after watching them for a few minutes he set off, moving around the perimeter of the ravine, searching for more sentries.

A hundred yards away he found the next pair. Men. Swarthy features. Arabs. Both carrying some sort of copy of the KK MP5 submachine gun.

Brenner-wolf skirted the two men and continued. Around the other side of the ravine, he came across the third set of sentries. Americans. Both kitted out in full private tactical response gear. Body armor, night-vision goggles. Camelbak hydration units. Both carried Glock sidearms and Sig Sauer submachine guns with suppressors.

Continuing his traversal of the ravine, Brenner-wolf arrived back at the Chinese encampment.

Six men. Chinese, Arabian, and American. Obviously working together but just as obviously separate. Different weapons, different kit. And just as obviously guarding something.

The wolf snuck down into the ravine.

A tent. Military issue. Large enough to stand in. Big enough for at least six people. Maybe more. Off to the right, a latrine pit.

Inside a bare flicker of light. Well concealed.

The wolf crept around the tent. Sniffing. Listening.

Two men. Talking softly. Russian.

Another smell. Lighter. Feminine.

Brenner-wolf found a small hole in the canvas and peered in. The two men sat at a folding table. They were playing cards. On the far side of the room, away from the door, there was a row of camp beds. A young girl sat on one of them. She was chained to the legs. Brenner could see her eyes were puffy from crying and her one cheek was red and swollen. Her lower lip was split, and the wound was starting to scab over. Mute evidence to her having been struck with a heavy hand.

The wolf ghosted back into the night, climbing out of the ravine then laying low, close to the first set of guards.

Brenner had been tempted to simply attack, as soon as he had seen the young girl. But caution had prevailed. So instead, he thought the situation through.

It was clear the girl was being held against her will. The chains bore testimony to that. It was also obvious it was vitally important to someone that the girl not get away. Or, perhaps, that no one rescue her. Whatever, she was surrounded by a group of heavy-hitters that looked as though they had been picked by the League of Nations. So, some type of international spy ring? Drug dealers?

Actually, thought Brenner. It doesn't matter who they are. A little girl is in obvious danger. *Ipso facto*, she has to be saved. I am here, *QED*, I will save her.

Satisfied with his logic he formulated a quick plan of attack. Kill everyone, take the girl to safety.

Done.

With his less than complex plan in place, Brenner morphed silently into Wolfman mode, stood upright and moved toward the Chinese bivouac.

Shifting in and out of shadow, he simply stepped into the foxhole, grabbed both the guard's heads and smashed them together.

Two down, six to go.

The Arab contingent was next. He crawled to the lip of their trench and was about to spring, when some sort of sixth sense caused the one guard to swivel his head. He stared directly at the Wolfman.

Brenner struck, his knife-like claws severing bone and gristle and tendons, separating the man's head from his body. The next swipe took the other guard in the chest, punching through to his heart, killing him almost instantly.

Almost. But not quickly enough to prevent him emitting a single strangled cry before his life was extinguished.

Brenner swore under his breath. The whole operation had just increased from a difficulty factor of three to one of nine. Because there was no doubt the Americans would now be on the alert. And if they were, then they may have communicated with the Russians in the tent.

Shit.

The Wolfman moved toward the pair of Americans. He had to be extra careful because he had seen they had advanced night-vision goggles. And Brenner knew, despite his amazing capacity to heal, being sprayed with a magazine full of 9mm ammunition would put a serious dent in his ability to carry out the rest of the mission.

He lay still for a while. At what he considered to be the edge of the safe perimeter around the Americans. Then he morphed back to human form and stood. Slowly. His hands above his head.

He was banking on the fact a large, butt naked man, walking around in the desert by himself, would baffle, or at least confuse, the guards. Until he could get a little closer to them.

To add to the surrealism of the scene, the big man decided to hum a tune as he walked. He chose the nursery rhyme, Three Blind Mice and started humming.

That way there was no chance even the most paranoid of sentries could suspect they were being attacked.

And sure enough, they took the bait.

They both stepped out of their trench. The one broke right, keeping Brenner covered, while the second guard walked up to him, his submachine gun held ready to use.

'Hey, boy,' he said. His accent a strong Southern drawl. 'You some kind of simple, or what?'

Brenner stopped walking but continued to hum the nursery rhyme.

The guard motioned with his weapon, pointing it at the ground. 'Down on your knees, boy. Keep your hands above your head.'

'Why?' quipped the second guard. 'You scared he's got a concealed weapon.'

They both sniggered.

Brenner got down on one knee, laced his hands behind his head and waited.

The first guard walked slowly around him, shaking his head in bewilderment.

'Well, what the hell do we do with this?' he asked.

The second guard shrugged. 'No idea. Maybe one of us should take him to the tent. Make him the Russian's problem. First, we better check on the other guards. See what that noise was.'

'Okay, I'll take him to the Russkies. You check on the others. Radio them first.'

The second guard nodded his agreement and started to take a small portable radio from his webbing, walking toward the closest foxhole as he did so.

As he passed close to Brenner, the big man morphed instantly into his Wolfman form, springing to his feet as he did so.

The change was so rapid, and unexpected, the two guards stood rooted to the spot, their brains too overloaded to allow any decision-making process to take place. They simply stared at the apparition in front of them.

In fact, they stared at it for the rest of their lives.

Then the Wolfman headed for the tent.

And the young girl.

CHAPTER EIGHT

Brenner hadn't left as wide a path as usual. Solomon had tracked the Wolfman before, and usually he was as subtle as a brick to the head. But now he was traveling with Griff, his passage was not as easy to follow.

There are very few six-foot-five, three-hundred-pound men riding across the country on black Harley rat bikes. But there are countless Americans cruising the highways and byways of the country in a Winnebago.

Also, it appeared there were no current photos of Reece Griffin. In fact, there was no public record of the man at all. It seemed as though he had decided to drop off the radar and live off the grid. And he had the skills to achieve his goal.

But Solomon had the vast machinery of the United States Army behind him. Limitless quantities of dollars and boundless man hours that could be brought into play with a mere phone call.

It didn't take him long to get a hit. It was a long shot, but Solomon reckoned it was worth taking a closer look.

It appeared a sheriff's office in the town of Pepperpot, West Texas had taken in a vagrant who had somehow managed to escape by single-handedly smashing his way out of a high security cell. Then the vagrant had proceeded to trash the building and attack the officer on duty. The doctor's report on the deputy had likened the man's injuries to those sustained from a major car accident. Like he had been driven over by a Mack truck.

After that, the vagrant had evaded capture and subsequently disappeared altogether.

The incident had Brenner written all over it.

Solomon grinned. The stupid bastards had probably picked the Wolfman up on the eve of a full moon. They were lucky he hadn't taken out the entire town. Killed every single person in an orgy of primeval destruction.

Not that anyone would have cared. Hell, the town was so insignificant it wasn't even on the map. But still, they had no idea how close they had all come to being totally annihilated.

Sergeant Solomon gave Howard the coordinates and the driver punched them into the SatNav.

Then Solomon pulled out his briefcase, selected a syringe of the red serum and plunged it deep into his neck, shuddering as the chemical concoction coursed through his veins. Keeping him alive another day. Bolstering his speed, strength, and healing to superhuman levels.

'Where are we going?' asked Lenny.

Solomon closed his eyes and lay back in his seat. He didn't bother to answer the massive slab of humanity sitting next to him. What was the point. It was like addressing a wall.

And sergeant Solomon didn't talk to walls.

CHAPTER NINE

It was obvious no one had warned the Russians, and they had not heard anything. Both were still seated at the table, playing cards. Brenner noticed they were using the Russian thirty-six card deck as opposed to the standard American fifty-two cards. He wasn't sure what game they were playing but it involved a lot of arguing and banging the cards down on the table with great force.

Whatever it was, Brenner was pleased they were playing it, as it took up most of their attention.

The Wolfman worked his way silently around to the side of the tent closest to the guards. His plan was simple. Slash through the tent, dispatch one of the guards then question the other.

Without further delay, Brenner struck. The canvas of the military tent parted like tissue paper under his claws and he leapt through the opening with a single bound. Swinging hard he sliced through the top of the closest guard's head, causing it to fly into the air like a Frisbee, spilling his brains onto the card table as he fell forward.

The young girl started to scream in terror.

The second guard stood and went for his pistol, drawing and raising it. He was fast, but not fast enough.

The Wolfman grabbed the guard's gun hand and squeezed. The sound of breaking bones was audible over the young girl's high-pitched scream. Then Brenner twisted hard, shattering the man's right arm. Casually switching his grip to the left, he broke that as well. Then he pushed the guard back into his chair, essentially incapacitating him.

'Don't be scared' he said to the screaming girl. 'I am here to help. I'm one of the good guys.'

But unfortunately, his oversized jaw, extra-long canines, and massive chest made his voice sound like Darth Vader on steroids. A deep rumbling growl, full of clashing teeth and heavy breathing. About as comforting as a personal message from the angel of death himself.

The girl stopped screaming, but only because her terror had ramped up to such a level, she had almost stopped breathing.

Brenner turned back to the guard. 'Who are you?' he asked. 'Who do you work for and why are you holding this girl captive?'

The Russian sneered at him. '*Trackhat tebya*, dog person.'

Brenner couldn't speak Russian, but it wasn't difficult to deduce the man was swearing at him. 'Now that's not nice,' said the Wolfman. 'I'm going to give you one last chance to talk. Then, time to die.'

'You will kill me anyway,' said the Russian. 'You are an evil spirit; death is always the outcome with the *Oboroten*.'

'*Oboroten*,' repeated Brenner. 'Is that a werewolf?'

The Russian nodded.

'Well, you see,' continued Brenner. 'I'm not actually a werewolf, so that changes things, doesn't it?'

'Yes, sure,' grunted the Russian. 'And I am actually Saint Nikolas. If it looks like *borscht* and it tastes like *borscht,* then it's usually fucking *borscht.* You're a werewolf. Now just finish it, dog-person, I won't tell you anything. Fuck you and fuck your bitch mother and all your dog-family.'

Brenner stared at the Russian for a few seconds then he nodded. 'Fine.' He leant forward, grabbed him by the neck and shook, snapping it like a twig.

The girl found her breath and started to scream once more.

Brenner morphed back into human mode and she stopped abruptly, staring at the naked man in front of her.

Eventually she spoke. 'You've got no clothes on.'

'Correct,' agreed Brenner as he stripped a blanket from one of the camp beds and wrapped it around his waist like a sarong.

'That's better,' mumbled the girl. 'So,' she continued. 'Antonev was right, you're a werewolf.'

'Not really,' answered Brenner.

'Yes, you are,' the girl insisted. 'I just saw you. So, are you going to eat me?'

'No,' said Brenner. 'I'm going to take you home. You're safe with me.'

She nodded. 'Good. My name's Cloe.'

'I'm, Brenner.'

'Have you got a car or something, Brenner?'

'No. We're gonna have to walk out of here. And we better get going in case some more of these reprobates pitch up.'

'Okay. How far?'

'Maybe four miles.'

'Shit,' exclaimed Cloe. 'That's far.'

Don't cuss,' commanded Brenner as they left the tent and clambered up out of the ravine.

'Why not?' asked Cloe. 'Don't you believe in freedom of speech? You some sort of communist werewolf? Anyway, it's just words. If I said sugar you would know I meant shit. So why be hypocritical?'

'You swear again I'll bite your right arm off.'

'Wow, you so won't,' denied Cloe. 'Anyway, calm down, grandad.'

'Hey, just how old do you think I am?'

'Dunno. About twenty-seven.'

'Close enough,' admitted Brenner. 'So that's old, is it?'

'Yeah.'

'Wait till you meet my friend, Griff. He's real old.'

'How old?'

'About a hundred.'

'No shit?'

'Hey, Cloe. Arm, remember?'

'Oh, yeah,' retorted Cloe. 'Of course, the whole eat-my-arm thing. I better stop cussing.' She smiled and her whole face lit up. 'Hey, thanks for saving me, Brenner.'

'No worries, Cloe.'

'So how much further?'

'Still four miles.'

'Can't you, like, change into a wolf, and I could ride you?'

'No. I'm not a horse,' grunted Brenner.

'Pity. Horses are cool'.

'So are wolves.'

'True.'

They trudged onwards into the night. After another ten minutes, Brenner picked her up in his arms.

She fell asleep almost immediately and the big man started to run, heading for the Winnebago.

CHAPTER TEN

The man woke slowly, his head throbbed like the worst hangover ever. His mouth was sandpaper dry and his eyes felt inflamed to twice the size. Like they were about to fall out of their sockets.

He sat up. An unfamiliar bed. Double. Relatively comfortable. A room. Large. No paintings on the walls. No furniture. A single, low watt bulb hung from the central light fitting.

The windows were boarded up. Full sheets of thick plywood fixed directly to the walls.

An open door that led through to an *en suite*.

Another door. Closed. He stood and tried the handle. Locked.

He walked through to the bathroom, turned the faucet on and drank until his belly felt swollen. His eyes started to water, and he started to sweat as his dehydrated body registered it now had been rehydrated to the point it could start to regulate its temperature once more.

He heard the door to the bedroom open and he turned to face the man who entered.

He was short and wide. Shaved head. Dark eyes, ill-fitting suit with no tie.

'Ah, professor,' he greeted. 'You had us worried for a while. Thought we may have inadvertently given you an overdose. We were about to call a doctor. But here you are, up and about. Fantastic.'

'Who are you?' asked the man. 'Where am I? Did you kidnap me?'

'So many questions, professor. Look, it doesn't really matter who I am, or where you are. The thing is, yes you have been kidnapped. Now, you didn't ask the most important question, why? Why are you here?'

'Well then, why am I here?' asked the man.

'That's simple. You are here to give us the precise formulae and manufacturing processes of your new enzyme conversion cocktail.'

The man snorted. Affronted. 'In your dreams. You can't strong-arm me; I stick by my beliefs. So, with all due respect, I must decline. Now, let me go and we shall talk no further of this.'

The bald man burst out laughing. 'Oh, professor,' he said. 'You genuinely think you are in a position to refuse us, do you?' He shook his head. 'Man, you academics, no grasp of the real world. You should have seen this coming. We made you a more than fair offer, you decided, in your arrogance, to turn down. So now, offer time over. Time to give us the goods, professor, or suffer the consequences.'

The man stuck his skinny chest out and set his chin. 'Go ahead, you thug. Do your worst.'

Baldy stopped laughing and stared at the professor. Then he winked. 'We will, prof, we will. The pain that we will cause.' He shook his head, as if even he could hardly believe the depths they were going to plumb. Then he smiled. A large, patently false grin. 'But not on you, professor. No. It would be real stupid for us to do damage to our prize asset.

Fortunately, you see, we don't need to. Because, we have your daughter.'

The professor went pale. His legs buckled, and he sat on the bed, all his resistance destroyed in one fell stroke.

Finally, he spoke. 'I don't believe you.'

'Yes, you do,' answered the bald man.

'Prove it.'

'With pleasure, prof.' He took out a cell phone, consulted the screen and selected a number, his face set in a supercilious smirk.

The two men waited while the phone connected and rang. Over a minute passed then the ringing stopped. The bald man frowned redialed and waited again until the phone cut out. Then he searched frantically through his menu and dialed another number.

They waited. The same thing happened. He tried a third number.

Finally, he dialed a fourth.

When no one answered, his face grew paler than the professor's.

Without a word, he dialed a fourth number, leaving the room and shutting the door behind him as he did.

And in an office in another state a man in a Stetson picked up his cell and answered.

'What the fuck are you phoning me directly for? I told you, this number is for the direst emergencies only, and I don't see no mushroom-shaped nuclear clouds on the horizon.'

'No one is answering, sir,' blurted the bald man. 'I've tried all four phones. They ring. But no one picks them up.'

There was a long pause before the man in the Stetson reacted.

'Shit.'

'Yes, sir,' agreed the bald man.

'Wait for my come back,' snapped the man in the Stetson. He disconnected then made a call.

Within minutes an H225 Super Puma helicopter was travelling out at speeds in excess of two hundred miles an hour. Heading for a tent hidden in a ravine in the middle of nowhere, Arizona. Looking for a young girl, and eight heavily armed mercenaries.

CHAPTER ELEVEN

Brenner lay the still sleeping girl on the bed, took her shoes off, and covered her with a blanket. Then he went outside, leaving the door to the Winnebago open so he could keep an eye on her sleeping form.

Griff lit two cigarettes, handed one to the big man. 'Okay,' he said. 'What gives?'

Brenner told him. He left no details out.

Neither man spoke for a while afterward. Griff mulled the situation over, rotating the problem in his mind, seeking out the whys and the wherefores.

Brenner smoked three more cigarettes.

'Well, we can't go to the cops,' said Griff.

'Why?' asked Brenner. 'I would think that's exactly what we need to do. Drop the girl off, wash our hands of the whole thing. Job done.'

Griff shook his head. 'Eight men, Russian, Chinese, Arabian, and American. The Chinese, at the very least, were carrying government issue, Special Forces weapons. This smacks of some sort of black ops, international cooperation. Joint task force of some type. Maybe government, maybe private. Factor in the kidnapping of an innocent girl and, well, let's just say, you report this. I guarantee within an hour you'll have a bunch of whack-jobs looking for you. CIA, Homeland Security, or worse, one of those departments that no one has ever heard of.'

'You don't reckon you may be just a little bit paranoid?' asked Brenner.

'So speaks a man running from Project Bloodborn.'

Brenner shrugged. 'Okay. You're probably right. What do you suggest?'

'We wait for the girl to wake up. We question her. That's the only place to start.'

Brenner nodded his agreement and lit up yet another cigarette, thankful his supernatural constitution protected him from their ill effects.

***

Brandon Taylor threw his Stetson to the floor and stamped on it.

'Say again,' he yelled. 'All dead.'

'Affirmative, sir.'

'How? Snipers?'

'No, sir. They look like … well … sort of, broken, sir.'

'Sort of broken? What the fuck does that mean, soldier?'

'Not sure how to explain it, sir. Never seen the like. Looks as if someone took a sledgehammer and smashed them up. Bashed in skulls, shattered arms and legs. Except for the last one. The Russian. Looks like someone took a sword to him.'

'A sword?'

'Yes, sir.'

'So, what you are telling me, is that a medieval warrior with a war hammer and broadsword killed my men and took the girl?'

The soldier didn't answer.

'Is that what you are saying?' insisted Taylor.

Again, there was no answer. There was no possible answer to give.

'You fucking imbecile,' shouted Taylor as he disconnected and threw the cell against the wall. The phone remained obstinately intact, so he ran across the room, picked it up and threw it again. This time it shattered with a satisfying crunch.

Then he went to his desk to get another phone.

He had many calls to make.

CHAPTER TWELVE

Cloe took a sip of the coffee Griff had just brewed and grimaced. 'What you make this out of?' she asked. 'Engine oil.'

The old man raised an eyebrow and glanced at Brenner. 'So, tell me,' he said. 'Why did you risk our lives saving this girl?'

Cloe grinned, and once again Brenner was amazed at the transformation that took place when she did. Her face went from sullen to angelic in a heartbeat. He wondered if she knew just how powerful her smile was.

'Sorry, Griff,' she said. 'Didn't mean to snap. It's just I've had a rough day, what with being kidnapped by armed terrorists then rescued by a werewolf.' She batted her eyes then looked down, her face a picture of contrition.

'*She knows,*' thought Brenner to himself. And he hid a grin at Griff's reaction.

'No, no, my darling girl,' said the old man. 'If you want some hot chocolate then you just ask ole Griff and he'll make some.' He walked over and patted her awkwardly on the head. 'You warm enough?' he asked. Uncomfortable in the extreme with having to take care of a person under the age of … he glanced down at Cloe. 'How old are you?' he asked.

'I'm nine,' answered Cloe. She saw the look of panic on Griff's face. 'Hey, don't worry,' she continued. 'I'm like highly intelligent. Seriously, I've got an IQ of 142. If you adjust that by age, its off the charts. Also, my mom died when I was young, and I've been homeschooled, so I can pretty much take care of myself. Trust me, I'm not a problem.'

Brenner could see that, although she was being flippant, Cloe was actually worried Griff might cast her out, such was his reaction to her age.

'Hey, Cloe,' said the big man. She looked at him and he winked. 'You're one of us now. Golden. And we stick together, no matter what.' He glanced at Griff who nodded.

'Together, no matter what,' he repeated.

Cloe said nothing. She simply took another sip of her industrial strength coffee. But Brenner could see the slight glaze of controlled tears in her eyes. And he felt for her. She was young, had no idea what was actually going on, and was stuck with two unknown men in the middle of nowhere.

'Right,' said Griff. 'First things first. Being a certified genius, I assume you remember your dad's numbers. Home and cell. Let's phone him and tell him you're safe.'

Cloe shook her head. 'No good,' she said. 'The Russian. Ivanov. He told me they already got my daddy. I told them my daddy was going to come for them and they better be scared. And he said, we already got the nerd in custody, so shut up.'

Griff took out his cell and turned it on. 'We try anyway. Maybe he was lying. Cell first, then home, then work. What's your dad's name.'

'James,' answered Cloe.

'Cool. And your surname?'

'James.'

Griff sighed. 'His first name?'

'James James,' snapped Cloe. 'His first name and his last name are the same. Don't ask me why, ask his parents.'

Griff smiled. 'So nice they had to name him twice.'

A few minutes later, Cloe's information had been confirmed. The cell was obviously switched off, the home phone rang until cut off, and the receptionist informed Griff the professor hadn't come to work for the last two days.

The old man put the phone back on the table, leaned back in his chair and thought for a moment.

Brenner lit a cigarette then started to prepare some food, rummaging in the cupboards for tins.

'Do you mind?' said Cloe. 'Ever heard of passive smoking? Secondhand smoke is actually more dangerous than firsthand smoke.'

'Wow,' said Brenner. 'That's terrible. Tell you what, whenever I light up, you better go outside. Can't take any chances with your health. Better safe than sorry and all that.'

Cloe scowled and was about to make a choice comment when Brenner reminded her.

'No cussing, remember?'

'Sugar,' she snapped. 'And fudge.'

'If you two children are quite finished,' said Griff.

Both Brenner and Cloe had the decency to look vaguely embarrassed at their behavior and turned their attention to the old man.

'Both Cloe and her dad were taken,' stated Griff. 'However, they weren't kept together. Now, there is only one reason I can think of why they would do that.'

'Coercion,' said Brenner, as he started to chop onions, and fry them in butter.

Griff nodded. 'They want something from the dad, so they keep them separate, threaten him by threatening harm to Cloe, and at the same time don't run the risk of the whole operation been compromised if one of the victims escapes or is discovered.'

Both of the men turned to look at Cloe.

'Right then,' said Griff. 'What exactly does your dad do? I heard from the phone call I made that he works for a place called the Global Green Research Group. What do they do?'

'All sorts of save-the-planet crap,' answered Cloe. 'Global warming research, rain forest, natural cures, alternative fuel production. Sorta a huge think tank for green ideas. He's a doctor of microbiology. To be honest, I'm not a hundred percent sure what he was working on. We're close enough but he doesn't discuss work with me.'

'Doesn't make sense,' said Griff. 'If he worked for the government, maybe. Even some sort of bio-chemical place, could be a weapon related thing. Any chance he was doing research on the side?' continued Griff. 'You know, doing work for the government? Perhaps the military?'

'No ways,' answered Cloe. 'Not my dad. He's like a super-green pacifist. Doesn't even eat meat. Neither do I, I'm a strict vegan.'

'Oh hell,' said Brenner. 'I've just finished cooking this. Corned beef, tinned sweetcorn, fried onions, bacon, and toast.'

Cloe laughed. 'Well, I'm a strict vegan when I'm at home with my dad. Anyway, bacon doesn't count.

Everyone knows that.' She accepted a plate from Brenner, smothered it in ketchup and started to eat.

While they ate, Griff fired up his computers and went to work, his fingers flying across the keyboards, lighting up the screens and causing a waterfall of facts and figures to cascade down. He would stop every now and then to shovel some food into his mouth, chew, and burp.

Every time he burped, Cloe giggled.

Brenner shook his head, a slight grin on his face.

Then Griff stopped, his fork halfway to his mouth. Replacing the fork, he turned to Brenner. 'Problems,' he said.

'Why?'

'What do you know about the production of cellulosic ethanol?'

Brenner grimaced. 'Let's assume I got a few gaps in my knowledge when it comes to cell … cellular … that stuff, and take it from there.'

'Cool. You know what ethanol is?'

'Yep,' affirmed Brenner. 'It's moonshine.'

Griff laughed. 'Could be. It is alcohol. Basically, the ethanol you're thinking of is made from distilling fruit. I'm talking about cellulosic ethanol, which is alcohol made from cellulose. Wood, grass, stuff like that.'

'What's it taste like?'

'It's not made for drinking, silly,' butted in Cloe. 'Cellulosic ethanol is made for fuel. Cars.'

'What she says,' confirmed Griff. 'And the thing is, dudes have been making fuel from cellulose for a while now, but its real expensive so it's not actually viable for commercial use. Now, it looks as though Cloe's dad has developed a single organism that can both break down the cellulose, and convert the resulting sugars into ethanol. It's like two hundred times cheaper than preexisting methods. In short, it's about half the price of gasoline.'

Brenner nodded his understanding. 'I get it. But why is that such a problem to us?'

'Just think, when this goes public, what do you think will happen to the oil companies?'

'I assume their share prices would take a dive,' answered Brenner.

'They would freefall,' confirmed Griff. 'Anyway, I've checked out James' emails. It seems as though he owns the patent on a personal basis, something to do with the contact he has with the Global Green Research Group. Looks like the company acts as an umbrella, but each researcher owns their own intellectual property. Long story short, all the oil companies have offered James a fortune to sell them the rights to the formula. I'm talking annual turnover of small country amounts here. But he's turned them down. Says the knowledge is for the people. Save the world, hug a tree, knit your own yoghurt, and so on.'

'That makes sense,' said Cloe. 'In fact, the only people my dad hates more than the government are the oil companies. Calls them, Satan's Spawn. And I agree with him.'

'So do I, honey,' agreed Griff. 'But the thing is, you can't refuse big oil without a price. These guys are more powerful than governments, richer than most countries and more ruthless than any dictator you've ever heard of.'

'So, they kidnapped me to put pressure on my dad,' stated Cloe.

Griff nodded. 'And it explains the whole, league of nations thing. My best guess would be that the top oil companies have got together to combat what they perceive as their greatest threat. They could easily do it single-handedly, but if they consolidate, they avoid fighting each other, and show a united front. Sort of an oil-driven Glasnost.'

'What you're saying is that we are now, most likely, in the crosshairs of the wealthiest, most amoral, ruthless bunch of corporations on the planet and they'll be coming for us with everything they have,' said Brenner.

'As I said before,' continued Griff. 'Problems.'

'What do you recommend we do?' asked Brenner.

Griff raised an eyebrow. 'Need you ask? We do what we always do … we find these fuckers and show them the error of their ways. With extreme prejudice.'

Brenner smiled. 'Works for me.'

Once more, Brandon Taylor turned to face the three foreigners. The Russian, the Chinese, and the Arab.

He had a new Stetson on.

And for the first time he was happy this operation had not been solely American. Because now the loss of the professor's daughter was a group failure, as opposed to a one-hundred percent all-American fuck up.

He had already told the group of the unfortunate loss of the package.

Now they were busy arguing and attempting to apportion blame on each other. He allowed them another ten minutes then he brought a halt to the mudslinging.

'Enough,' he commanded. 'Blaming each other is counterproductive. Let us accept joint responsibility and rather spend our efforts on finding out who did this, whom they work for, and whether we have a leak in our group.'

Lin Yang shook his head. 'In China, we do not have traitors,' he said. 'All Chinese work for the glory of the state and the people. It is unthinkable.'

'What he said,' added Oleg, the Russian. 'We have no traitors. We killed them all a long time ago.'

Fadil Ali said nothing. He knew well how corrupting vast sums of money could be to anyone, no matter how scared they were, or how indoctrinated.

Taylor had held his hand up. 'I'm not saying any of us is a Benedict Arnold. But it just might be one of our people has strayed from the path. Tempted, as it were. However, we have a bigger mystery to solve first.'

With a push of a button the drapes swished closed and a white screen unreeled from a cavity in the ceiling. The lights dimmed, and a series of pictures appeared on the screen. Like stop motion photography. One image every three seconds.

Black-and-white. Night time. Taken from high angle. On the side of the screen, a scale line to give an idea on the sizes of the objects they were looking at.

'Gentlemen,' said Taylor. 'These are sequential satellite images taken last night over Arizona, one every three seconds. These are the actual photos of our package being stolen. The image is using infrared so, as you can see, the whereabouts of all the people are clearly visible.'

The images were slightly blurred but, considering the distance and the fact it was night, it was remarkable they could see anything at all.

In the center of the screen was the tent, nestled in shadow at the bottom of the ravine. Inside, three distinct splashes of white. Two large, one small. The body warmth of the people inside showing up.

At the edges of the ravine, three sentry posts. Two people in each. Once again lit up by the infrared.

Then a bloom of light appearing on the very periphery of the screen. As one, all glanced at the scale line on the side. Quick calculations were done.

'What the hell is that?' asked the Russian.

'Person?' ventured the Arab.

'It's huge,' countered Oleg.

'Big person, maybe,' said Lin Yang.

'Yeah,' agreed Oleg sarcastically. 'A person the size of an ox.'

The next photo showed the bloom of heat had moved. Now it was next to the first sentry post.

'Wait,' said Oleg. 'How did it get there so fast? These things refresh every three seconds. If you look at the scale, from the edge of the screen to the guards is well over seven hundred meters. Almost eight hundred yards. Nothing moves that fast.'

The next photo shuttled onto the screen. Now the large body of light was between the first and second sentry post.

The first sentry post showed the same two patches of light. The two guards. Except it was obvious they were fast cooling. Their body warmth dropping. Mere gray blobs as opposed to bright white.

Cooling rapidly.

As corpses are wont to do.

Then the next photo. Then the next.

Nine seconds had passed, and all six sentries were dead.

The thing that had done it was now in the ravine. Next to the tent.

The four onlookers held their breaths. They all knew the outcome, but somehow, they found themselves hoping against hope. The thing lay still for two more photos.

Oleg broke the silence first. 'Get out,' he whispered to himself. 'Get out now, while you still can.'

The next photo showed the thing was inside the tent.

Nine seconds later the thing was at the top of the ravine. Next to it, a tiny patch of light. The girl.

Then they were gone.

The satellite tracked with them. Losing them in some shots, capturing them with others.

The pair became one. Obviously, the thing had picked the girl up. Then, once again, it moved faster than humanly possible.

The satellite caught up again some miles further on.

Some sort of small building. Another person appeared. Then the screen went blank

'That's all we could get,' said Taylor. 'The orbit moved on. Our lab boys say the small building was actually a Winnebago recreational vehicle. Not sure of the model. We have the coordinates, but I've already sent a helicopter there and there was no trace of them. Nothing within a hundred miles either. These boys are good.'

'What the fuck were we just watching?' asked Ali. 'Is this for real?'

Taylor nodded.

'Nothing that big moves that fast,' argued Oleg. 'In fact, nothing alive moves that fast. Is there a problem with the download information? Are you sure that was all in real time?'

Again, the Texan nodded. 'Look, boys. Let's just say, we have no real idea what that was. Could be a fucking tiger for all we know, that doesn't matter. What matters is we no longer have our asset, and without it, our lives become more difficult.'

'Perhaps we don't need the girl,' ventured Lin Yang. 'I have some particularly gifted men who could question the professor. I am sure they would extract the required information.'

Taylor nodded. 'Yes, Yang,' he agreed. 'We too have some of those people. However, in the past we have found certain people do not react well to torture, be it physical, mental or chemical. Particularly left-wing academics with real belief. Eventually we can break their spirits, but often we find we break their minds in the process. And we need the professor's mind to be one hundred and ten percent intact, and willing to work for us. This invention of his is too important to take any unnecessary risks. Later, perhaps, if all else fails, then we can get more brutal. But at the moment, let us concentrate on finding the daughter.'

'I have a question,' said Ali. 'Why don't we just kill him? Problem solved?'

'That is a viable option,' agreed Taylor. 'But it's definitely the very last one we'd want to use. After all, we want that formula. Oil can't last forever, and it would be nice if we had the alternative ready and waiting, wouldn't it?'

There was a round of laughter and agreement.

'Excellent,' said Taylor. 'Now, let us put together a task force that can track down whatever this was that took our property and eliminate it.'

CHAPTER FOURTEEN

Howard had deliberately driven slowly, timing their arrival to coincide with the setting of the sun.

His timing was perfect. They cruised into the no horse town of Pepperpot as the sky changed from red to deep indigo. There was no one on the street, but that looked as if it were the norm, as opposed to the fact that night had just fallen.

The sheriff's office, however, was still well lit. Outside were three white Crown Vics and an Explorer. Solomon knew that even in a no-happen place like Pepperpot, the law normally stayed late. Or at least the bulk of it. Howard pulled up outside the offices, got out and went around to open Solomon's door for him.

Lenny got out himself, clutching at his head as he did so.

'What's your problem?' asked Solomon. 'Why you pawing at your head?'

'Pain,' mumbled the man-mountain. 'Sometimes my head hurts real bad.'

'Well stop pawing at it. You look like a gorilla. Man up.'

Lenny nodded; his eyes red-rimmed with pain.

'You watch the car,' Solomon told Howard.

'You sure you won't need backup?' asked the driver.

'What, in this place? You jest, I'm sure,' quipped Solomon as he strode up the stairs and opened the main door, Lenny shambling behind him.

He walked up to the charge desk and rapped on it to attract the attention of the man standing behind it. 'Sheriff Harris,' he said. 'Fetch him. Now.'

The deputy behind the charge desk didn't even deign to look up from the computer screen in front of him.

Solomon knew the drill. Small town. Run clean and hard by the local cops. When addressing the local law, then every sentence was expected to be prefaced with either a 'sir' or 'deputy' or 'sheriff'.

He was having none of that. 'Lenny,'

'Sir?'

'Smash this chap's face in. Try not to kill him.'

The deputy looked up with a jerk as he heard Solomon's instructions, but it was too late. Lenny leaned over the counter, coiling his arm around the man's neck and, as fast as a striking snake, whipped his face down and into crushing contact with the surface of the charge desk.

There was a wet thud as the deputy's face was almost turned inside out, such was the power of the hit. Lenny let go, and the lifeless body slid to the floor.

Solomon shook his head. 'Lenny, Lenny, Lenny. What did I just say?'

'Try not to kill him.'

'And what have you just done?'

'Sorry, mister Solomon, sir.'

Solomon patted the mountain on the arm. 'That's okay, Lenny. We all make mistakes. How's your head?'

'Still mighty sore, sir.'

Another deputy ran across the room, drawing his pistol as he did so. 'Hey,' he yelled. 'What the hell just happened here?' He pointed the weapon at Lenny. 'Put your hands above your head.'

'Calm down,' said Solomon. 'We're here to see sheriff Harris.'

The deputy looked down at the fallen body of his comrade, noting the pool of blood and the misshapen skull.

'Jackson,' he shouted. 'And Pope. Front desk now.'

Two more deputies came running from the back of the open plan offices, both drawing their weapons as they did.

Lenny rubbed his head and mumbled to himself. Solomon looked bored and simply stood still, his eyes focused on the middle distance. Vacant.

'Both of you put your hands on your heads,' commanded the first deputy. 'Do it now.'

'Sheriff Harris, please,' repeated Solomon, his voice matching his bored demeanor.

'I said put your hands on your head,' screamed the deputy, his finger tightening on the trigger.

'Solomon sighed. 'I do not know why I bother being polite. Really, I don't. It's actually a bit of a character flaw, if truth be told, I'm just too nice to people.'

'This is your last warning,' shrieked the deputy.

There was a plop of imploding air. Like a champagne cork being released. Then Solomon was standing behind the deputy. He grabbed his arm with his right hand and twisted hard, at the same time, snatching his firearm away with his left.

Pulling the deputy backwards he used him as a shield, keeping him between himself and the two other armed men.

Solomon grinned. 'Too slow,' he said as he flipped the pistol into the air, caught it by its barrel and swung hard, casually crushing the deputy's skull with one quick strike. Then he picked the deputy up and threw him, one handed, into the other two.

'Catch.'

The pair fell as the corpse crashed into them.

'Butterfingers,' taunted Solomon. 'If you want to catch someone, you have to watch the body into your hands. It's no good taking your eye off. You'll always fumble that way. Anyway, I'm going to talk to sheriff Harris. I assume he's in his office. Lenny. Incapacitate these two. Again, I say try not to kill them. Restraint, old chap. Restraint.'

With a blur of movement Solomon was outside the sheriff's door. Another flicker of light, the door had been thrown across the room and the man in black was sitting on the edge of the sheriff's desk.

To sheriff Harris it looked as though the stranger had simply materialized out of thin air whilst an invisible tornado had snatched his door off its hinges and taken it away.

Solomon stuck his hand out. 'Sheriff Harris, I presume.'

The sheriff stared blankly at the proffered appendage. 'What the fuck?'

'What the fuck indeed,' agreed Solomon. 'Oft my exact sentiments.' He grabbed the sheriff's hand, shook it, and stood.

Behind him, in the open plan office, Lenny had a desk and was proceeding to turn it into kindling by smashing it against the remaining two deputies' prone bodies.

Harris went for his sidearm but all he got was empty holster. He looked up to see the stranger in black holding his weapon.

'How the hell did you get that?' he asked.

'Not important,' answered Solomon. 'Now sit, sheriff. We need to talk.'

'What's that thing doing to my deputies?' shouted Harris.

Solomon looked back at Lenny who was still beating the deputies with the remains of the desk. 'Lenny,' he called. 'Remember. Restraint. There's a good boy.'

Lenny put the remnants of the furniture down and stood still, his face expressionless.

'There you go,' said Solomon. 'He's stopped. Now, let's talk.'

Harris didn't look ready to talk. In fact, his eyes were wild, and he looked readier to run. Or maybe have a massive coronary. 'What the hell is going on here,' he whimpered as he fell back into his chair.

'Just a few questions,' said Solomon. 'Sorry about the deputies. I tried to be polite, but they were disinclined to return the favor. I guess they just aren't used to treating the general public with anything approaching respect. So, obviously I had to discipline them. I'm sure you understand, being the sheriff and all.'

Harris' face had gone slack as his ability to process the situation he was in totally overrode his current skill set.

'A couple of weeks back,' continued Solomon. 'You and your redneck deputies arrested a man. Not sure why, don't care. Long and the short of it, he busted out of your jail, broke one of your deputies and absconded. Is that correct?'

Harris stared at Solomon like he had grown horns.

'Come on, sheriff,' snapped the man in black. 'Concentrate. Week or so back. You arrested a man. Stranger, you remember?'

Harris nodded.

'Good.' Solomon held out a photo. Old. Brenner in Vietnam era camouflage. Helmet on his head. A pack of Lucky Strike cigarettes in the band. 'Was this him?'

Again, the sheriff nodded.

'Well done, sheriff. Now, where did he go?'

Harris shook his head. 'Don't know, mister. We tried to track him, but it was just like he disappeared into thin air.'

'And that was that,' said Solomon. 'He almost kills one of your deputies and you just let him go?'

'No, sir,' denied Harris. 'We kept searching for a few days. Didn't find nothing.'

'A few days,' repeated Solomon. 'And such was the worth of your deputy. A few days.' Solomon shook his head. 'Why did you stop?'

'Told you, sir,' repeated Harris, his eyes on the floor. 'There weren't nothing to find.'

Solomon sighed. 'Now, Harris, I don't know much about shit-eating small towns like this. I try my hardest to avoid them, you see, I'm allergic to stupid. But I do know one thing. You good ole boys don't stop searching for someone who harmed one of your own just because you got bored. Why did you stop? And be honest now, or I might get Lenny to break a few desks on your head.'

The sheriff went pale and his right eye started to twitch.

Solomon chuckled. 'Don't tell me, let me guess. Did this have something to do with a very, very large wolf?'

The sheriff's look of surprise was comical. 'How did you know?'

'I know many things,' said Solomon. 'Now, tell me the story, and be succinct, I've wasted enough time in this shithole already.'

'We arrested the stranger because we suspected he had come to spy on the Pastor's set up,' said the sheriff. 'And the Pastor paid us all well to protect his investments. But that night he busted out, beat up on Dexter, the man on duty, and split. So, we tried to track him down. Couldn't find him. The next thing it all went to shit. We heard he had killed the Pastor and gave his farms to the workers or some such thing. Then before I could investigate, I had a visitation.'

'A visitation?' asked Solomon. 'You mean, as in the appearance of a divine or supernatural being?'

The sheriff nodded. 'That would be the one, yeah. One of those.'

'Who was it?' asked Solomon.

'It was the tribal ancestors. And the moon wolf. It was real, I tell you, sir. I could feel the beast's breath on my face. The ancestors told me to fuck off and never look for them or the stranger again and to stay clear of the farms … or else. Then the wolf damn near bit my face off. I passed out and when I woke up there was no trace of them. I swear,' stressed the sheriff. 'I ain't no crazy man. I swear to the Lord it happened. Anyhow, I stopped looking, called the search off. Still can't sleep at night. See those teeth, snapping at my face. Can still hear the howl.' Harris shook his head and Solomon could see the man was close to collapse. 'I saw the face of the dark angel,' he whispered. 'And I shall never know peace again.'

Solomon stood. 'Where are these farms you mentioned?'

Harris pointed. 'That way. Leave the town and head north-west. There's basic tracks. No roads. You'll find it. There ain't nothing else out there.'

Solomon put the sheriff's pistol down on the table. 'Here,' he said. 'If I were you, sheriff,' he continued. 'I'd use this to shoot myself. Because if I know that wolf, and I do, he's coming back for you. Maybe not next month, or even next year, but one day, you'll look up and he'll be there. Then he's going to rip your face off. Bye now, and thanks for the info.'

The man in black walked out, stopping at the two prone deputies Lenny had laid out. He sighed in disappointment. 'Lenny, I said restraint. And look at this, you killed them both.'

Lenny shook his head. 'No, mister Solomon,' he said. 'That one's still alive.' He pointed at the body on the left.

Solomon bent down and checked the man's pulse. It was there. Barely, but there was a light ragged beat. He smiled as he stood. 'Well done, Lenny. Extremely well done.'

Lenny grinned like a loon. 'Thanks, mister Solomon. I tried my best.'

Solomon patted the man mountain in the back as they left the building.

And behind them, sheriff Harris picked up his pistol, slipped off the safety, and placed the muzzle against his temple.

CHAPTER FIFTEEN

The Winnebago headed west. Toward San Bernardino. The home of Cloe and James.

After a few hours, they hit the outskirts of the town and headed for the north-western suburbs.

On the way in they drove past the MacDonalds Museum, situated on the site of the first MacDonalds.

Griff shook his head. 'Dudes, look at that,' he said. 'A shrine to mankind's subjugation of taste and good food.'

'I like Mickey-dees,' argued Cloe.

'Thought you were a strict vegan,' contended Griff.

'MacDonald's don't count,' stated Cloe. 'Same rules as bacon.'

They pulled into Mount Pleasant Street. Tree lined. Midrange houses, slightly worn. Three to four bedrooms, single garage, two-point-four children, two family pets, one cat, one dog, most likely a Labrador.

Cloe pointed. 'There, at the end. The pink house.'

Griff drove past the house, slowing down marginally as he did so to take a cursory glance.

'See anything?' he asked.

Cloe shook her head.

Brenner nodded. 'Single male, top floor. Arabic features. Tweaked the drapes as we drove past.

Possible movement first floor but can't be one hundred percent sure. Odds are there are at least two of them, more likely four. Most probably B team, just in case someone of interest pitches up.'

'You saw all that?' said Cloe. 'Man, what are you, superhuman or something?'

'He's definitely or something,' confirmed Griff as he turned the corner and parked the Winnebago some two blocks away from the house. 'You want to wait until dark?' he asked Brenner.

'Yep. Let's get something to eat. Come back after sunset. I'll go in first, neutralize the threat, then bring Cloe in. She can stock up on clothes, see if she can find anything that might amount to a clue.'

Griff nodded his agreement. 'Okay, Cloe,' he said. 'This is your neck of the woods. Where should we go to eat. Not MacDonalds, and not some tree-hugging vegan hangout.'

'Got just the place for you,' replied Cloe. 'Perfect eats for meat fascists such as yourself. Drive, and the vegan guide shall show you the way.'

And two hours later they were back in the vicinity of Cloe's house. She had been correct about the restaurant. An Australian themed steak house that had served up a platter suitable for men with Brenner's appetite for red meat. Griff had a smaller portion of the same and Cloe stuck to her seemingly arbitrary vegan rules and had a tofu burger with a side of bacon.

They sat silently in the Winnebago. The sun had gone down around half an hour before, but Brenner wanted to wait.

After a while, Griff fired up one of the computers and let Cloe play a few games. Brenner polluted the atmosphere with secondhand smoke and Griff drank a soda.

Finally, Brenner stood. 'It's time,' he said as he opened the door and left, heading for Cloe's house.

The young girl watched him walk away. Then she blinked, and he was gone.

CHAPTER SIXTEEN

Abdul was bored. The four men had been staying in the house for three days, and there was little to do to break the monotony. At first, he had welcomed the assignment. A few days with no chance of danger, sitting back drinking sweet tea and soda, eating takeout food and watching American cable television.

No such luck. It turned out the professor obviously did not believe in television as an acceptable form of entertainment. It wasn't that he didn't have cable, he didn't even have a television. And there was a limit to how much crappy western pop music one could listen to before going mental. He had tried talk radio but that was even worse. Godless heathens complaining about their perceived problems while some shock DJ insulted them in return. Didn't they know all could be solved if they just bothered to read the Quran?

No wonder his brethren wanted to destroy the Americans. They were louche, weak, and Godless.

Fazil and Gamil had already turned in and it was up to himself and Hadid to take the next twelve-hour shift. Another twelve hours of butt clenching boredom. He sat on the sofa and opened the holy book at random. At least he had the Quran.

As he started to read, he heard a sound outside the back entrance. Almost undetectable. Like a leaf brushing up against the door.

'Hadid,' he called out. 'That you?'

'Is that me what?' answered Hadid.

'I thought I heard something at the back door.'

'Not me.'

'Go and check,' said Abdul. 'I'm reading The Book.'

There was a sigh from the dining room and Abdul could hear Hadid walking over to the kitchen.

'See anything?' asked Abdul.

No one replied.

'Hey,' he called out. Did you see anything?'

Still no response.

Abdul stood and moved toward the kitchen, drawing his pistol as he did so. He walked into the room, weapon ready. The back door was open. And on the floor, surrounded by a pool of blood, was Hadid's headless corpse.

Before he could react, something tore his pistol from his grasp. He turned to face his foe only to find himself face to face with a monster from *Jahannam*.

A *Jinn* from the very fires of hell itself.

'*Ya, Allah*! Help me, God,' screamed the Saudi.

The *Jinn* reached out and grabbed him by his face, its claws encircling his head. 'How many others are there?' it growled at him, its voice as foul as the sound of a million sinners burning in the fires of hell.

'Two more, upstairs,' replied Abdul, as he shook in terror.

'Are you sure?'

'I swear it.'

The beast picked him up and, with one sharp jerk, snapped his neck. Then it proceeded upstairs.

***

Brenner had changed back and wrapped himself in a sheet, like a toga. Then he had covered the two bodies in the kitchen with blankets. There was another corpse upstairs and, sitting on a chair in the lounge, the fourth guard.

Griff had gone upstairs with Cloe and they had packed a small suitcase with her goods. Now all stood in the lounge, facing the prisoner.

'Cloe,' said Brenner. 'Take your case and go and wait in the Winnebago.'

'Why?'

'You don't have to question everything,' replied the big man. 'Just do it.'

Cloe nodded and left, taking her suitcase and heading for the vehicle Griff had parked in the driveway.

Brenner waited for her to go before he addressed the Saudi.

'Right, question time. Let's start with, who do you work for and where is James?'

La ilaha illa Allah. Mohammadun Rasulu Allah.'

'What?'

'He said, there is no god but Allah and Mohammed is his messenger. Or something close,' said Griff.

Brenner raised an eyebrow. 'How do you know all this stuff?'

Griff shrugged. 'I'm old. Knowledge just seems to come with the territory.'

'I'm also old,' countered Brenner.

Griff shook his head. 'No, my friend. You've simply been young for a very long time. It's different, trust me.'

'Whatever. Now listen, dude,' said Brenner to the Saudi. 'You had better answer the questions or things will go bad for you. But if you answer truthfully, I will let you live. This is a once only, limited time offer. Understand?'

'*Allahu Akbar.*'

'He said …' started Griff.

'Yeah, I know that one,' snapped Brenner. He stared at the Saudi for a few seconds then he laughed. Mirthlessly. 'Fine,' he said. 'Have it your way.'

And he exploded into Wolfman form. The sheet shredded as his body mass went from two hundred and seventy-five pounds to over four hundred. His head smashed into the overhead light in the middle of the room and his growl shook the very foundations of the house.

'Talk!' snarled the Wolfman as he held his razor-sharp claws in front of the Saudi's face.

The man in the chair seemed to fold in on himself as his fear overcame his religious strength and he started talking almost immediately.

'I work for Fadil Ali. Aramco. Saudi oil. But I've only ever met him once. I don't know exactly where the hostage is. I swear. Somewhere in Las Vegas. A private residence. That's all I know. Please don't eat me.'

'Why do they always say that?' asked Griff. 'As if being eaten is worse than just being killed.' He looked at Brenner-Wolfman as he spoke. Noting well the claws, the teeth, the massive jaw. And he shook his head. 'Yeah, actually, I get it. Stupid question.'

'Let's go,' growled Brenner as he stalked from the room.

As they got to the door, there was the sharp retort of a gunshot, and a bullet struck the Wolfman high up on his back. He spun around to see the Saudi was holding a small two barreled Derringer. He fired again, and the slug hit Brenner in the chest.

The Wolfman shook his head. 'Now, why did you have to do that?'

He strode over and grabbed the man by his neck.

The Saudi stared at him for a second then whispered. 'Mercy?'

'Sorry,' answered Brenner as he broke the man's neck. 'I'm all out.'

Sheriff Harris had been correct. It didn't take Solomon long to find the farm. He headed north-west and within half an hour, his supernatural eyesight had picked up the glow of electric lighting on the horizon. A beacon in the desert.

Howard pulled over about a mile from the source, and the three of them had continued on foot. Solomon and Lenny were unarmed but Howard carried a Glock pistol in the 10mm range, and a Heckler and Koch 337, compact assault rifle chambered for the .300 whisper round. Enough firepower to knock down a charging bull elephant.

There was no fencing around the farm buildings, but there were two sentries. More like lookouts than guards. They were armed with shotguns, but the weapons were slung over their shoulders as they walked.

The area was well lit, and Solomon could make out acres of soya, pumpkins, and sweet potatoes. On the one side of the buildings was a row of motorbikes and a well-maintained Ford Ranchero pick up. He could hear lively discussion. Laughter.

Solomon gestured to Lenny and Howard to stop and wait as he blurred into motion. There was a couple of sharp retorts, and the two sentries lay still on the ground, necks twisted at impossible angles.

Lenny shook his head as Solomon rejoined them. 'No restraint.'

The man in black frowned. 'Don't be stupid, Lenny,' he said. 'I meant to kill them. Never leave armed men at your back. It always ends in tears. Now come on, let's see who's who in this zoo.'

Solomon led the way. The door to the main building, a single story, prefab hall, was open. The three strangers entered, Lenny bending down and turning sideways to fit through.

The hubbub of chatter stopped as all eyes turned to face them.

There were around twenty plus people in the hall. Predominantly male.

A long refectory table filled most of the room and all were seated around it. On the table were jugs of fruit juice. There was no alcohol.

Solomon did a quick scan of all present and immediately picked out the leaders. An elderly native American man and a younger woman, most probably in her late twenties. They were seated next to each other at the far end of the table. He addressed them directly.

'Good evening. My name is Solomon Hopewell. The man holding the assault rifle is my assistant, corporal Howard. And that monstrous lump of flesh behind him is called Lenny.' Solomon walked over to the native American and the girl. 'And you two are?' he asked.

'I am chief Kohana Harjo,' replied the native American. 'And this young lady is doctor Materia Santiago. What do you want with us?'

Solomon took out his photo of Brenner and showed it to them. 'This man. When was he last here, and where is he now?'

Both Kohana and Matty looked at the photo then shook their heads.

'Never seen him,' said Matty.

'That's an old photo,' pointed out the chief. 'We wouldn't recognize him now even if we had seen him.'

Solomon sighed. 'Lenny,' he called out.

'Mister Solomon, sir?'

'Lenny, do me a favor and break one of the young men at your end of the table.

Lenny took two fast steps, grabbed a young native American male by his arm, pulled him from his chair and threw him against the wall.

The man struck the wall so hard the plaster fell off and a long, jagged crack appeared in the masonry. His body hit the floor like a sack of wet newspaper. Completely boneless and unmoving. It was plain to all the man would never move again.

As one, the men around the table started to stand.

But Howard fired a quick burst of automatic fire into the ceiling then trained his weapon on them.

'Sit,' he commanded. And all obeyed.

Solomon showed Matty and Kohana the picture again. 'Take another look,' he urged. 'And, if it makes you feel any better, we are not here to harm sergeant Brenner, we are merely here to take him home. You see, he's been gone a while and we truly do miss him. Now, try again, and do hurry, before I feel that Lenny may have to provide a little more encouragement.'

Kohan glanced at the doorway before he looked at the photo again.

Solomon laughed. 'I hope you weren't expecting your sentries to come bursting through the door at any time,' he said. 'Because if you are then you shall be waiting for a very long time. A very, very long time.'

Matty went pale as the actuality of what Solomon was saying struck home. He had been there less than a minute and his presence had already resulted in the death of three men.

'You monster,' she said through gritted teeth.

Solomon nodded. 'Regrettably, yes,' he agreed. 'The photo?'

'He was here a couple of weeks back,' said Kohana. 'He didn't stay long. When he left, he didn't tell us where he was going. He simply left.'

'Howard,' commanded Solomon. 'Shoot someone in the eye.'

The flat retort of the assault rifle sounded in the room, and a woman halfway down the table flew backwards off her chair in a spray of blood.

Solomon raised an eyebrow. 'You shot a girl,' he noted as he shook his head. 'Cold, Howard. Ice cold.'

Howard shrugged. 'Male, female. Dead is dead.' He trained his rifle on the rest of the people, his expression hard. No one dared move.

Lenny shook his head. 'That's not right,' he said. His voice a disapproving rumble. 'You shouldn't shoot girls.'

'Lenny, shut it,' said Solomon. Then he turned to face Matty. 'Talk, doctor,' he said. 'That last death was on you. How many more do you want on your conscience?'

A tear slid down Matty's cheek and she took a shuddering breath. 'He was here two weeks ago. He had a friend with him. An older man named Griff. They stayed for a while. Sorted some things out. Some problems. Then they left. As far as I know they were heading for Dallas. Griff said he was picking up a new Winnebago there. Said it was a special, not your normal run of the mill vehicle. I think I heard him mention someone called Weasel. When they left, Griff was driving a dark blue Range Rover. Brenner rode his bike. A black Harley. Not sure what year. That's all we know, I swear.'

Solomon nodded. 'I believe you.' He stood and turned to Howard. 'Corporal,' he said. 'Kill them all.'

'No,' screamed Matty as she launched herself off her chair and grabbed Solomon by the hand. There was a huge bang, and a flash of blue-white electricity that threw both Matty and Solomon to the floor. The air stank with the smell of burning flesh and Solomon's suit jacket smoldered and smoked.

He stood and stared open mouthed at Matty who was struggling to her feet.

Solomon held up his hand. 'Howard, belay that order. Wait.' He peered closely at the doctor. 'What the hell did you just do?' he asked.

Matty shook her head. 'I don't know. I just wanted to stop you killing everyone. It isn't necessary. We are not your enemy. We mean you no harm, we were simply trying to protect our friend.'

Solomon didn't answer. No one moved. The room was silent.

'Brenner is your friend?' Solomon asked.

Matty nodded.

'But he is a killer. A monster. His default setting is to attack. Why would anyone befriend that?'

'Because he means well,' answered Matty. 'Everything he does, he does for the better good of all. He protects the weak. He rails against injustice. And most important of all, he fights the monster inside him. You say his default setting is to attack. You're wrong. His actual default setting is to kill. To kill without mercy and without end. But he resists. He forces himself to be a better being. He has compassion.'

'He has no sense of duty,' said Solomon. 'And a man without a sense of duty is merely an animal. As for compassion. It's overrated. However, just this once, I shall show some. Come on, Howard, Lenny. Let's go.'

The three men left the building.

As they walked away, Matty heard the big one ask a question.

'Hey, mister Solomon. Your eyes are blue. How come your eyes are blue now? They were black before that girl electrified you?'

'I don't know, Lenny,' answered Solomon. 'I truly do not fucking know. Now shut up, okay?'

'Yes, mister Solomon.'

CHAPTER EIGHTEEN

Vegas is bigger than people think,' said Griff. 'Everyone just thinks of the Strip. And maybe Downtown. But there are over two million people living here, or in the close surrounds, on a permanent basis. And that isn't counting the over one hundred thousand daily visitors. In fact, it covers over one hundred and fifty square miles. That's a lot of houses.'

'Well, we better start looking,' said Brenner. 'Where should we base ourselves?'

'The Bellagio,' answered Cloe. 'I've heard it's awesome.'

'In your dreams,' laughed Griff.

'Why not?' asked the young girl. 'It isn't as though you can't afford it. I've seen that suitcase full of cash under your bed.'

'Don't go snooping around my place,' snapped Griff.

'Hard not to,' retaliated Cloe. 'it's one room and we're in it all the time. Would be nice to get a suite with a couple of rooms at least. And a nice bath, and food that isn't based on fried corned beef.'

'Hey. Griff,' said Brenner. 'You always say it's only money. What the hell. Let's book a suite at the Bellagio. At the very least, no one would think of looking for us there.'

Griff shook his head. 'Bloody heathens. Right, fine. Let's do it.'

Cloe squealed with excitement.

***

'One thousand five hundred dollars a night,' said Griff as he threw his rucksack down on one of the beds in the master room of the two-bedroom, lake view suite. 'And they don't even throw in free parking. Highway robbery.'

'It's just money, dude,' said Brenner.

'Wish I'd never said that,' grumbled the old man as he took out his laptop and fired it up. 'At least they have free Wi-Fi,' he conceded.

'Can I order room service?' asked Cloe.

'Pass the menu,' said Brenner. 'Let's have a look.' He scanned the offerings and blanched. 'Man, these guys charge like a wounded grizzly. The burger costs more than my first car did. No way. There's a limit to what I'm prepared to shell out for bread and meat, even if it is just money. Tell you what, let's go out for a bite.'

Griff shook his head. 'You two go. I'm doing some online detective work here. I'm going to attempt to find a link between any of the oil companies and any properties listed in Vegas. Shouldn't be difficult, I'm sure they won't have even bothered to hide it. Why would they? They didn't expect anyone to come looking. Also, I'll check anything that's just been rented in the last few days, particularly if it's been for cash or by some obscure offshore company. It's all a long shot but we have to start somewhere. Order me a steak sandwich and a couple of beers.'

Brenner complied, then he and Cloe left in search of a place to eat that didn't involve wheelbarrows full of cash.

They ended up going to the in-house buffet. It was under thirty dollars each and Brenner was able to eat his own weight in rare steak. Cloe had sushi.

'You do know that sushi doesn't qualify as vegan,' Brenner pointed out.

'Veganism is a state of mind,' answered Cloe. 'One just has to remember, animals are our friends, not our food.'

'A fish is an animal.'

'Don't really wanna be friends with a fish,' admitted Cloe. 'Look, the important thing is, I try.'

Brenner shook his head and laughed. 'Come on, finish up and let's get back to the room. See what Griff has turned up.'

CHAPTER NINETEEN

Griff had narrowed the search down to five residences. Three were rented by subsidiaries of Exxon, one had ties to Aramco and another had been charged to a company Griff was pretty sure had connections to a Russian oligarch who was well connected to the oil industry.

'Good work,' said Brenner.

Griff shook his head. 'It's a crap shoot. I did a surface search. We're talking four of the biggest companies in the world. If I really went deep, I would probably find at least another two or three hundred properties that were allied in some way to one of them. But I reckoned we start at the shallow end of the pool and wade on in. At least we get someplace to start and some people to question. Shake a few trees, see what falls out.'

'Right. Cloe, stay here,' said Brenner. 'You okay with that?'

'No complaints from me,' answered the young girl. 'I'll Have a two-hour long soak in the tub then veg out in front of the TV. You guys have fun knocking on doors.'

Brenner suggested they rent a car as opposed to driving around in a forty-three-foot-long twelve-foot-wide home on wheels. But Griff had disagreed. The hassle of the drive was worth the added firepower and computing power it brought with it.

The first two residences were in the suburb of Summerlin. It was obvious from the outset that neither was their target property. The first had three young children playing ball outside and the mother was visible through the sitting room window as she kept a close eye on her children. Brenner skirted around the back of the property and peered into the windows that were easily accessible. It was a typical family home.

The second was empty. No furniture. Nothing. A quick circuit revealed all and they moved on.

The third property was in Henderson, which felt like a suburb of Las Vegas but was actually its own town, complete with separate police force. This property was set back from the road. A low wall surrounded it and a row of mature trees screened the front entrance.

'This looks a little more promising,' noted Brenner. 'Locked front gate. Drapes are all pulled. No sign of life, but two vehicles parked in the driveway.'

'You wanna wait until nightfall?' asked Griff.

Brenner shook his head. 'We don't know what sort of time frame we're up against. Might be that every second counts. I think I'll sneak around the back. Give it the once over. You got any more of the in-ear comm links?'

Griff swiveled his seat and pulled one out of his desk drawer.

'Here. Remember, it'll work even if you go Wolf-man.'

'Thanks,' said Brenner as he climbed out of the Winnebago.

Griff watched him walk away and marveled as he simply seemed to disappear into the hedges and shrubbery. The incredible vanishing man. Over two hundred and fifty pounds of invisible.

***

Karl Peterson was an ex-military sniper. As such, boredom was a way of life to him. Any good sniper knew waiting was a large slice of the job. But even he was starting to feel jaded.

He had been lying in wait, on an exposed flat roof in the Nevada sun for a week. Staring at a bungalow style residential home. Knowing the chances of anything happening were so close to one hundred percent as to make it inconceivable.

But the package they were protecting was a level-one. In his business, that meant any and all measures had to be taken to protect and secure the area.

And if that meant they had to place eight heavily armed guards in the residence, six more on standby, connected via a panic button and a sniper on a roof close by to provide overwatch, then so be it. The old adage, better safe than sorry, had never been more apt.

Karl stifled a yawn and peered through his scope again, scanning the bungalow and surrounds.

The hair stood up on the back of his neck. A man. Tall. Well built. Karl concentrated. Somehow, even in the late afternoon sun with very little cover, the man was managing to remain semi-concealed. He used the shadow like it was a cloak. Blending rather than hiding.

And Karl knew, anyone that skilled could only be a professional. He flicked the safety off his rifle, raised himself up onto his elbows, and took a deep breath.

The receiver crackled to life in Brenner's ear. One word.

'Drop.'

Brenner didn't hesitate. He hit the ground and rolled. Fast.

Above him a lump of plaster fell from the wall and a slug ricocheted above his head.

'Sniper. Your eight o'clock,' snapped Griff. 'Move to the south side of the building. Now.'

Brenner followed directions, running hard.

'Sniper is down,' said Griff. 'I've taken him out. Bloody amateur, let himself get silhouetted. Sorry about that, Ded,' he continued. 'I only spotted him as he was about to take the shot. Not sure if he warned the others or not, but you got two choices. Either you leave, or you go in hard, right now.'

'I'm going in,' replied Brenner as he smashed through the back door.

Two men sat at a kitchen table. Both wore shoulder holsters. On the table were the makings of a couple of major sandwiches. Pickle, turkey, ham, lettuce, mayonnaise. Next to the fixings were two Remington pump-action shotguns.

Before the men could react, Brenner grabbed the one shotgun and used it as a club, smashing left and right. Both men fell to the floor and the big man finished each of them with a swift stamp to the neck.

He had been shot at and these men were armed. *Id est*, all here were the enemy and must be treated as such.

He burst through into the corridor and jinked left through the first open door.

Sitting room. Three men. All armed.

Shotguns boomed. A submachine gun joined in, chattering insanely as it filled the air with lead.

Brenner leapt forward and jumped behind the sofa. There was the sound of ripping cloth.

And from the other side of the sofa appeared the Wolfman.

There was a brief pause in the barrage as the three men in the room tried desperately to reconcile what had just emerged from behind the sofa, with the human being that had disappeared behind it.

The Wolfman took advantage of the lull in the gunfire and bound forward, maw open wide and claws at the ready.

The man with the submachine gun managed to get off three shots on full automatic. A quarter second burp of sound.

The two shotgun wielders were both dead before they could even squeeze their triggers. Blood spraying across the room, headless torsos falling limply to the floor.

Brenner grabbed the machine gun carrier by the face, tearing the weapon from his hands as he did so. 'How many more?' he growled.

The man pulled a knife from his belt and stabbed the Wolfman in the chest, grunting with the effort. 'Fuck you, whatever you are,' he shouted.

Unfortunately for the knife man, the blade barely penetrated the Wolfman's super-dense muscle and bounced off, skipping from the man's hand and falling to the floor. He stared at the knife, open mouthed with surprise.

'Wrong answer,' grunted Brenner. Still holding the man's face in his massive paw, he took two steps toward the wall, rammed his head into it, smashing it like an egg.

As he did so, the adjoining door flew open and another three men burst in. They took a split-second to assess the situation before deploying their weapons.

It was a split-second too long.

Foot long, razor-sharp claws cleaved flesh. Ribs were shattered. Lungs, intestines, and other sundry internal organs were released from their cages of muscle and bone to fall freely to the floor. Changing instantly from functioning organs to mere piles of dead meat.

And the Wolfman howled as he bathed in the blood of his enemies.

Moving swiftly, the huge creature headed for the corridor. Using his sense of smell, he left the first two closed doors and honed in on the last one. He paused outside, knowing at least one guard would be waiting for him to come through the door. If the guard had a shotgun, then that wouldn't be much of a problem. However, if he happened to be carrying an assault rifle, things could get mighty unpleasant. Even the Wolfman couldn't easily shrug off ten or twenty rounds of full metal jacket slugs traveling at over 3110 feet per second.

So instead of going through the door, Brenner opted to breach the wall next to it. He gathered his strength, braced himself against the opposite wall then, with two fast steps, crashed through, ducking and rolling as he did.

As it happened, there were two guards inside the room. One carrying a shotgun and the other sporting a Colt 1911. Brenner grabbed the shotgun by the barrel, yanked it away and struck the bearer in the neck, snapping his spine like a wooden chopstick.

The second guard managed to pull off two quick shots before the Wolfman's paw enveloped his hand and his pistol and crushed both.

The man dropped to the floor, squealing in agony.

Brenner cuffed him on the side of his head. 'Shut it,' he growled. 'You sound like a little girl. Where's James?'

The man stopped shrieking and took a shuddering breath as he stared at his mangled appendage. The barrel was bent around his thumb and his trigger finger was broken and twisted into the trigger guard. His hand had become an obscene sculpture of broken flesh and twisted steel.

He looked up at the Wolfman with an expression made up of equal amounts of fear and hatred. Then he tilted his head toward an interleading door. 'There,' he croaked. 'In the bathroom.'

'Are there any more guards?'

The man shook his head.

'If you are lying,' warned Brenner. 'Then I will crush every bone in your body. You will most likely live, but you will be crippled. A quadriplegic. Do you understand?'

The man nodded.

'Once more then,' continued Brenner. 'Are there any more guards?'

'I pushed a panic button just before you crashed into the room,' admitted the man. 'More soldiers will be here in a few minutes.'

'Good man,' said Brenner. 'You just saved your own life.'

'Fuck you,' breathed the guard.

Brenner-Wolfman grinned. A terrifying display of teeth.

Then he opened the bathroom door.

A man stood inside. Average height. Average build. Average everything.

'Mister James?'

The average man nodded. Brenner was impressed to see the man's expression more inquiring than fearful.

'I am a friend of Cloe's,' rumbled Brenner. 'She is safe. Please come with me.'

James nodded, and Brenner was pleased to note the scientist didn't bother with unnecessary questions. He appreciated the gravity of the situation.

As they were about to leave the room, Brenner stopped in front of the man with the broken hand. Then, with the swiftest of movement he slashed his throat.

He died without a sound.

'Never leave an enemy behind,' whispered Brenner to himself. 'Griff,' he continued. 'You hear me?'

'Loud and clear, good buddy.'

'Pick us up.'

'ETA two minutes. I'll honk.'

'Thanks.'

Griff drove fast but not recklessly. Brenner had warned him about the panic button and the imminent arrival of reinforcements, and he wanted to get as far away from the target area as possible before they arrived.

Brenner sat opposite James and Cloe. On the table between them were three cans of soda and a bowl of roasted peanuts. Cloe lay against her dad and held his arm as if scared he would suddenly disappear.

'Werewolves don't exist,' said James.

'I agree,' said Brenner. 'As I told you, I'm not a werewolf. I'm the result of a clandestine military experiment that attempted to create a super-soldier.'

James stared at the big man for a few seconds as his scientist's brain churned through all the relevant information available to him. 'But I saw you in said form,' he continued. 'Teeth, fur, inexplicably large muscle mass. That implies empirical proof. Therefore, werewolves do exist.'

'Daddy,' said Cloe. 'It doesn't matter. We're safe. Stop overthinking things, believe me, sometimes it helps to freewheel.'

'Are we safe?' asked James.

Brenner nodded. 'Safer than you were.'

'And I'm heading for a place that will make you even safer,' added Griff.

'Where is that?' asked James.

'You know the asshole of the world?' asked Griff.

Cloe sniggered but James simply shook his head.

'Oh, well,' continued Griff. 'This place is about ten miles further on. Near to Sugar Bunker. It's a former chemical explosives storage unit. Was also used for various seriously fucked up nonnuclear experiments during the nuclear moratorium. My friend lives in an abandoned mine some six or so miles from there. Basically, you get to Coyote Springs, take a left and keep driving until you hit hell.'

'And you want to take us there?' asked an incredulous James.

Griff nodded. 'Safe. I mean, no one else in their right mind would go anywhere near the place. And there's no danger from the chemicals and such what. I think.'

'You think.' said James.

'Does your friend live alone?' asked Cloe.

Griff thought for a while before he answered. 'Yes,' he said. 'And no.'

'Can't be both,' pointed out Cloe.

'You'd be surprised,' argued Griff. 'Look, the dude is a bit of a loner. He's an avid Prepper and makes my levels of paranoia look childish. His name is Dave Cornell. He was a lieutenant back in the day. Son of a wealthy industrialist type. After his parents died, he left the army and simply moved his life lock, stock, and barrel to this place. It's state of the art. If money can buy it, then Dave has it. As long as it's necessary to survive the forthcoming apocalypse. Whenever that arrives. Unfortunately, Dave has what is politely called, a few screws loose. Playing with a full deck, he is definitely not.'

'What do you mean?' asked Cloe in a worried voice. 'Like, criminally insane? Psycho? Cultist?'

Griff laughed. 'No. The thing with Dave is, he developed multiple personality disorder, most probably brought on by traumatic stress suffered in 'Nam.'

'So, he's schizophrenic,' said Brenner.

James shook his head. 'No,' he said. 'Contrary to popular misconceptions, people with schizophrenia do not have multiple personalities. In fact, delusions are the most common psychotic symptom in schizophrenia; hallucinations, hearing voices, stuff like that. The word "schizo" does mean "split," but Eugen Bleuler, who coined the term schizophrenia in the early nineteen hundreds, was describing the rupture in the person's thinking process and emotional response. Not developing another personality. What Griff's friend is suffering from is, dissociative identity disorder, also known as multiple personality disorder. It's a mental disorder characterized by at least two distinct and relatively enduring identities or dissociated personality states. Not normally dangerous to the sufferer or those around them.'

Cloe rolled her eyes. 'Geez, Dad. Lecture people much?'

James blushed. 'Sorry. I didn't mean to sound patronizing.'

'No worries,' said Brenner with a chuckle. 'It was informative. Thanks.'

The professor looked pleased at the big man's compliment and even Cloe managed a smile.

'So, who else is Dave, when he's not Dave?' asked Brenner.

'Thaddeus Meriwether Cornell,' answered Griff. 'Dave is pure redneck and Thaddeus is a Victorian gentleman. Just don't laugh. Act normal and all will be cool.'

James shook his head. 'This is all very strange,' he murmured to himself as he stared out of the window at the rolling red desert sands.

CHAPTER TWENTY-TWO

Once again, Howard's timing was impeccable. As he pulled up outside the chain-link fence that surrounded the premises they were looking for, the sun dropped below the horizon.

He got out of the car and went to open the back door.

Solomon stepped out, shot his cuffs and straightened his necktie.

Lenny clambered out of the other door, and the BMW suspension hissed and sighed as it was relieved of the four-hundred-pound burden.

The fence had a large gate in the front. Wide enough to accommodate an articulated truck and high enough to discourage any intruders. Rolled razor wire stretched across the top of both gate and fence, supported between two splayed pieces of steel.

The gate was closed and padlocked from the inside.

Solomon gestured toward it. 'Lenny. Open that.'

The huge man lumbered forward and, without slowing in the slightest, simply walked through the gate. Metal bent, buckled, then snapped as the industrial strength hinges were torn off the stanchions and the gate fell into the property, like a Tiger tank had just rolled over it.

'Thank you, Lenny,' said the man in black.

Lenny smiled and bobbed his head in pleasure at the approbation.

'Howard. Provide overwatch,' continued Solomon. 'Anyone tries to escape, stop them. Permanently.'

The driver nodded, leaned into the vehicle and took out his assault rifle.

Solomon strode toward what appeared to be the entrance to the building and Lenny trailed behind him. An elephant and its mahout. But before he got there, the door burst open and three men ran out. They were of a type. Dressed in blue overalls, grease stained, long hair, patchy beards, and questionable personal hygiene. They were all armed. One carried a large wrench, the other a length of pipe, and the third had a switchblade.

The switchblade carrier spoke first. 'Hey. You broke our gate.'

'How very observant of you,' said Solomon. 'Now we have that out of the way, I'm looking for Weasel. Go and fetch him for me, that's a good fellow.'

'You broke our fucking gate,' repeated the knife wielder.

'Yeah,' said one of the others. Obviously feeling that knife boy needed some moral support.

Solomon pinched the bridge of his nose and sighed theatrically. 'So,' he said. 'It's going to be one of those conversations. Why can't people just do as they're asked?' He shook his head. 'Go and fetch Weasel,' he repeated, talking slowly as if talking to a non-English speaker. 'And I feel it is only fair to tell you, this is your last chance to comply. If you don't do as you're told, then this shall surely all end in tears. And we don't want that, do we?'

The knife man was still staring at the flattened gate, puzzling out how the hell it had ended up on the floor when there was no bulldozer to do the damage.

'How the fuck did you break our gate?' he asked.

There was a blur of color as Solomon moved, then the man slowly keeled over and hit the floor. Sticking out of his forehead was the hilt of his switchblade, the rest was buried in his brain.

And Solomon was once again standing in the same place.

'Fetch Weasel,' he said to the wrench carrier.

The man nodded, dropped his wrench and ran back into the building.

The man holding the length of pipe also laid his weapon down and stepped back, holding his hands above his head like a prisoner of war.

Solomon ignored him.

Less than a minute later, seven more men came walking out of the building. The obvious leader stood in the vanguard. Skinny, hair in a ponytail, late-era Elvis sideburns, seventies porn-star mustache, and a set of teeth that telegraphed his nickname to all.

And these men were armed with real weapons. Pump-action shotguns, semi-auto pistols, and revolvers.

'Weasel, I presume,' said Solomon.

'Who the fuck do you think you are?' shouted Weasel.

Solomon raised an eyebrow. 'Oh, I know who I am,' he answered. 'But be that as it may, I'm looking for Brenner and his erstwhile companion, Reece Griffin.'

Weasel stared at the downed gate. Then at his downed compatriot. 'You broke my gate,' he said. 'And my man, Robbie.'

'Really,' sighed Solomon. 'Are we seriously going to go through the whole gate routine again?'

Weasel raised his pistol and pointed it at Solomon. 'Listen, pretty boy,' he said. 'You and me are going to go round and round for a while.'

Solomon shook his head. 'No,' he said. 'We are not. Lenny. Hurt these men. Badly.'

The man mountain launched himself forward. Arms held wide he simply rushed at the group of men. Shotguns roared, and revolvers cracked, but Lenny was amongst them before they could deal out any real damage.

People bandy about expressions like, a fox in a hen house, or perhaps, a bull in a china shop. However, watching Lenny attack Weasel's men was more akin to a combine harvester in a butcher's. Blood there was aplenty. And raw flesh. Shattered bones and dismembered torsos.

And, at the end, a pile of dead meat.

Weasel flinched as he witnessed the speedy and violent end to his men.

Then he recovered, turned his pistol on Solomon and pulled the trigger. But Solomon was no longer there. Weasel felt a sharp pain then he was sitting on the floor. Solomon stood over him, Weasel's pistol in his hand and a slight smirk on his face.

Weasel tried to move but a wave of pain crashed down on him, almost causing him to black out. He looked down at his right arm, and saw it was twisted at a ridiculous angle. As if it had been torn off and replaced by a being with no actual concept of the human body. His elbow bent the wrong way, his thumb lay back against his wrist, his fingers were as limp as boiled spaghetti and his shoulder had been so badly dislocated the right arm was two inches longer than the left.

'I'm looking for Brenner,' said Solomon.

Weasel started to talk but another surge of pain turned his answer into an unintelligible agonized whimper.

'Come on,' urged Solomon 'Don't have all night. Talk up.'

'You're a fucking bastard,' grunted Weasel.

'Yes,' agreed Solomon. 'And then some. Talk.'

'I have no idea,' rasped Weasel. 'He was here. He came with Griff. Never seen him before that. He's an asshole. Roughed up my boys and threatened me. I supplied them with their goods, they paid, they left. That's it.'

Without warning, Solomon cocked the pistol and shot Weasel in his left knee.

The buck-toothed man screamed in agony as he thrashed about on the floor, his ruined arm flopping about like a wet towel, and his shattered knee pumping out blood. Deep red and viscous.

'You can do better than that,' said Solomon. 'Brenner. Where?'

Weasel took a shuddering breath then spoke. 'I put a tracker in the Winnebago,' he admitted. 'I wanted to keep an eye on them. Wanted to get my own back at that arrogant fuck, Brenner. Came in here throwing his weight around like he owned the place. After

I tie up a few loose ends here I'm going to track him down and teach him a lesson.'

'How does it work?' asked Solomon.

Weasel pulled a cell phone from his shirt pocket and slid it across the floor to the man in black. 'It's an app. Works on the cell network. It's in the menu. It's called Worldtrack.'

Solomon picked up the cell, turned it on and scrolled through the menu. Then he grinned. 'Good.'

'Are you going to kill me?' asked Weasel.

Solomon nodded.

'Shit,' said the buck-toothed man. 'Lately I just can't seem to catch a break.'

Solomon laughed. 'Yep,' he agreed. 'Sometimes life just sucks.'

He shot him twice in the face, dropped the pistol and walked away.

CHAPTER TWENTY-THREE

The last couple of hours had been decidedly tedious. The Winnebago moved forward at a speed that barely exceeded walking pace, following a couple of ruts in the desert that Griff generously referred to as "the track".

Then they stopped.

In the middle of nowhere.

'Is this it?' asked Cloe.

Griff nodded. 'Close. It's somewhere there.' He pointed at the side of the large canyon they had been crawling down for the last couple of hours.

'I don't see anything,' countered the young girl.

'That's the point,' answered Griff. 'Anyway, I've sent Dave a message via the net, he knows we're coming so now we wait for him.'

Minutes later a quadbike seemed to appear out of the cliff face, heading toward them. It pulled up in front of the Winnebago. The rider got off and walked up to Griff who was standing in front of the RV.

He was of medium height. Well built, in a ripped, spare sort of way. His hair was long, graying, and tied back in a tight ponytail. Rough shaven but clean. His eyes were a dark blue and they were set off by large, thick eyebrows.

'Reece.'

'Dave.'

The two men hugged and banged each other on the back, laughing with pleasure as they did so. Then Griff turned and gestured for the others to join them.

Brenner climbed out of the Winnebago followed by Cloe and James.

Griff introduced them and explained James and Cloe needed to get off the grid for a while.

'Well then, you have come to the right place,' acknowledged Dave. 'I defy anyone to get more off the grid than I am. I'm so deep, even I forget where I am at times. Come on,' he continued, as he mounted his quadbike. 'Follow me.'

They trailed after him as he headed toward what looked like a solid cliff face. As they got closer, Brenner saw the entrance to what was obviously a large cave had been artfully camouflaged with netting and painted canvas that had been cut into strips and hung in front of it.

Dave rode straight through the camo strips and Griff followed him. They stopped as soon as they had passed the entrance. Griff switched off the ignition and they all disembarked.

Around them was a large antechamber that had been roughly hewn out of the living rock. Fifty feet wide, twenty high and around two hundred long. Strings of exposed low-energy bulbs were strung along the walls and at the far end of the chamber stood a sturdy double sized door set into the rock. It was closed.

Brenner scanned the chamber and picked out at least three cameras set into the roof. There were two alcoves on the right-hand side of the space. One contained an up-armored Humvee, complete with

.50 cal machine gun and the second alcove garaged another two quadbikes. The floor was made up of packed earth and swept clean.

There were no other entrances or exits.

Dave dismounted and gestured for them to stay with him. They followed him through the double doors. He closed the doors behind them, relocking as he did.

Brenner raised an eyebrow. They had fallen down the rabbit hole.

It was like entering a casino. Or maybe a small up-market cruise ship. The place was vast. A circular shaft, four stories high. The floor area at least two hundred feet in diameter. A stairway ran up and around the circular wall, creating a sweeping gallery with doors that led off it, into the heart of the living rock. On the far end of the cavern a glass elevator graced the wall. Chandeliers glittered, and water fountains hissed and gurgled. Vast arrays of leafy plants thrived under strategically placed lights, and the air was a comfortable seventy degrees Fahrenheit with a relative humidity of forty-five percent.

'Wow,' said Cloe. 'This place is super awesome.'

Dave smiled. 'Yes,' he admitted. 'It is pretty neat, isn't it? Come, let's get something to eat.'

The prepper led them to the elevator. They got in and he pressed the button to the fourth floor. The door at the rear of the elevator opened into a kitchen area. It wasn't huge, but it was large enough to have a twelve-seater table in the center and ample cookers and appliances. It was more an industrial affair than a domestic one. Stainless steel surfaces and glass fronted refrigeration units.

'I have enough food here to feed twenty people for two years,' said Dave. 'A combination of deep frozen and tinned. I also have a well, and a water recycling unit. Four generators, diesel for six years, guns, ammunition, computers, hazard suits, a full medical center, communications center, and hydroponic tanks for fresh vegetables. Everything has two and sometimes three separate backups.'

'Why?' asked James.

'The apocalypse, man,' answered Dave. 'End of the world, dude.'

'When do you think that's going to happen?' asked the scientist.

Dave stared at the academic like he had just grown an extra head. 'It's already happened, man,' answered Dave. 'It's already happened.'

***

Dave created a meal of more than adequate proportions for all. Beef steaks, fresh vegetables, and fresh water from the well. Then he had shown them all to their separate rooms.

Cloe and James elected to stay in the same room and they were left to their own devices to catch up and get used to what was happening to their lives

After that, Dave showed both Griff and Brenner to his study. A wood paneled room with leather Chesterfield sofas, book lined walls, and a large oak desk. He offered cigars, Cuban, that were accepted with thanks, and he clipped them before handing them over.

Then things got weird.

Dave lit his cigar, took a slow drag then turned to face Brenner, pulling his hair from its ponytail as he did so and letting it flow down past his shoulders. Then he took a monocle from his shirt pocket and screwed it into his left eye.

'Hand rolled on the thighs of a virgin,' he said to no one in particular, his Southern accent replaced by a clipped and haughty tone. Then he laughed. A high, braying sound. 'Absolute poppycock, of course. Makes for a good story though.'

He took another drag. 'So, I trust David has made you comfortable. Showed you your quarters. Had you fed and watered?'

'That he has, Thad,' answered Griff, with a warning look at Brenner.

'Please, Reece,' said the man who used to be Dave. 'I have asked you before not to call me Thad. My name is Thaddeus. To shorten it in such a will-ye-nill-ye fashion is to emasculate it in the extreme. Just will not do, don't you know?'

'Sorry, Thaddeus,' apologized Griff. 'Won't do it again.'

'Good chap,' approved Thaddeus. He turned to Brenner. 'Now, as for you, old man,' he said. 'I suspect David has no idea what you actually are.'

'And that would be?' asked Brenner.

'Oh, come now, a denizen of the night, of course. A *loup-garou*. A turnskin. A lycanthrope. Werewolf.'

Brenner thought before he answered, and he decided not to argue the point regarding whether he was a werewolf or an experimental super-soldier. Instead, he merely nodded. 'David doesn't know. I think.'

Thaddeus walked around Brenner, filling the air with blue smoke as he did so. Then he stopped and placed his hand on the big man's head.

Brenner didn't move.

Thaddeus closed his eyes and stood stock still for almost a minute. Then he let out a deep sigh. 'You are being hunted,' he said.

Brenner nodded. 'Always.'

'I see a vampire and a troll. They come for you. They seek to take you home.'

'I have no home,' said Brenner.

'Ah, yes,' said Thaddeus. 'A man who lives everywhere, lives nowhere. However, they see you as a brother. Bad tidings indeed. For the undead are so hard to kill, are they not? Cognac?'

Brenner blinked at the non sequitur then his brain caught up. 'Yes, please,' he said.

Thaddeus poured three brandy balloons of fine brandy and passed them around before he continued talking. 'Beware the Watchers,' he said.

Brenner smiled. 'What, those old dudes. Don't think I have any worries there.'

Thaddeus shook his head. 'Belittle them not,' he said. 'For they have more power than you credit them. Take heed, king of wolves, you exist only if you exist in their eyes. They are the ultimate proof of life.'

'Thaddeus,' said Griff. 'How come you know all this shit?'

'I pay attention,' answered the faux-Victorian. 'The news is there for all to read, but most choose not to recognize the writings on the wall.'

'Weird,' said Griff.

Thaddeus laughed again. A donkey at play. 'No more bizarre than a man who is also a wolf and also ...' he stopped. Tilted his head to one side. 'Much more,' he finished. 'But that is for another time and place. For now, I advise you speak to James James and seek out the men who were responsible for him and his daughters kidnapping. 'Tis time to discover the snake pit and stamp on the head of the viper that dwells there.'

***

Both Griff and Brenner had stayed up late the previous night questioning James then formulating a plan.

James informed them the man they were looking for was one Brandon Taylor. He would not be found on the Exxon company website and, if they asked, all knowledge of him would most likely be denied. The fact he was the most powerful person in the multinational enterprise was a detail known by very few.

As far as planning went, it was up to Brenner's usual standard. Find out where Taylor was, go there, use force to stop him and all those who helped him.

Vengeance boiled down and reduced to its most simple form.

As it happened, it didn't take Griff long to track Brandon Taylor down. Because, although he made no habit of shouting out his name and position, he also went to no lengths to hide.

He was currently in San Antonio, staying in a residence owned by a subsidiary of the oil company.

Griff figured it would take them at least twenty hours to get to the city, as he wanted to take the back roads to keep off the radar as much as possible.

The next morning, while they were gassing up the Winnebago, Dave came to them. He was carrying a large aluminum case. Placing it on the ground in front of Brenner, he clicked it open.

'I'd like you guys to take this,' he said. 'I know you're well-armed but I figure you won't have one of these and it's always been my belief you can never have too much firepower.'

Brenner picked up the weapon. It looked like four rocket tubes welded together with a shoulder mount and trigger mechanism.

'Never seen one of these before,' admitted the big man. 'What the hell is it?'

Griff finished up at the gas pump and walked over. 'It's a FLASH,' he said.

Dave nodded his agreement. 'FLame Assault SHoulder Weapon. Designated, M202A1. Features four tubes that can load sixty-six mil incendiary rockets. Each warhead contains approximately one and a half pounds of napalm. It's accurate enough out to five hundred yards. I've thrown in two salvos. Eight rockets in all.'

Brenner grinned as he put the weapon back into its case. 'I like it.'

They packed the FLASH in the gun cabinet with the other weapons and bid their goodbyes. Cloe gave each of them a kiss and James shook hands and thanked them once again for their help.

Three hours later they were out of the desert and back on something that resembled a road, travelling toward San Antonio. Six hours after that Griff decided to pull over and stop for the night. He drove off the road for a couple of miles then Brenner pointed out a perfect place to rest up.

Griff parked the Winnebago and opened a brace of beers while Brenner got to frying up his usual mess of corn beef and whatever other tin came to hand.

Later, after a few more beers, they went to bed.

They didn't bother to set up a sentry roster.

CHAPTER TWENTY-FOUR

Brandon Taylor placed the phone back on his desk and took a deep breath.

His head of security, Jonathan Briggs, an ex-black ops specialist, sat across from him. And he knew his employer well enough to see he had just received bad news.

'Mother. Fucker,' said Taylor. He enunciated each syllable. Putting as much feeling as possible into the words. 'Useless. Bastard. Mother. Fuckers,' he continued.

Then he stood, pulled a Colt Defender .45 caliber pistol from his shoulder holster, slipped the safety off, aimed at the seventy-two-inch television mounted on the opposite wall and pulled the trigger.

He fired until the magazine ran dry.

Eight shots.

Briggs didn't even flinch. 'Bad news, boss?'

'The sons of bitches got the professor,' answered the Texan. 'They just waltzed in and took him. Wall-to-wall bodyguards, sniper overwatch, a full backup team, and they just took him like they were a couple of teenagers out shopping.'

'Who, boss?' asked Briggs. 'We got a traitor in our ranks? Maybe the Russians. Could be the ragheads. Or those fucking Chinese, slant-eyed mothers, can't trust them.'

'You've just narrowed it down to everyone we're working with,' snapped Taylor. 'Great deductive reasoning, Briggs.'

'Truth be told, boss, I don't really trust any of them.'

Taylor nodded. 'Me either, me either. But it's not them. Our boys have done their forensic work already and given me the lowdown.'

'So, who do we need to kill, boss?'

Taylor shook his head. 'Honestly? None of the forensics makes real sense. We got fingerprints from the house and we got number plate recognition on the transport. We also got some CCTV footage and two eye witnesses that claim to have seen the driver. We got a match on the prints. According to military records they belong to a sergeant Ded, no middle name, Brenner. Excepting the fact he died back in Vietnam in the sixties. The Winnebago they drive around in seems to be driven by another ex-soldier, name of Reece Griffin. He's in his late seventies. As would be Brenner if he's still alive.

As well as that, they found lots of hair at the scene. Animal hair. Closest match they can get is that it comes from a wolf.'

Briggs frowned. 'So, we looking for two old men with a pet wolf driving around in a big recreational vehicle?'

'That about sums it up,' admitted Taylor.

'Shouldn't be that difficult,' offered Briggs.

Taylor snorted. 'You think? These two old men and their dog have taken out over twenty of our top operatives from four countries. And they did it without breaking a sweat. In fact, from what we can observe from the satellite info, one of them did it by himself. So, I would venture to say that it can, and will be, difficult, Briggs. Fucking difficult indeed. Now listen closely, we cannot afford any more fuckups here. I want everyone in on this. And I mean everyone. I will get hold of the Russians, Chinese, and Arabs. You mobilize all our guys. Then I want you to call every outside contractor that we have ever used. Even those mad South Africans. Everyone. Cost is no object.

I will use our police and FBI contacts to find these men. I also want you to put a reward out on the grapevine, tell everyone there is a million-dollar reward on their heads, dead or alive. That should get every lowlife bounty hunter and scumbag in America searching for these old men.

I want them killed, Briggs. And I want my professor back. Understand?'

Briggs nodded. 'Crystal, boss. Shock and awe.'

Taylor nodded. 'Shock and fucking awe, mister Briggs.'

Because he could see perfectly in the dark, Solomon drove the BMW for the last couple of miles without any lights. The tracker app on his phone showed they were close to the Winnebago that Weasel had put a tracker in.

When Solomon figured they were approximately a mile away he stopped, and they went the rest of the way on foot.

Howard carried his assault rifle while both Solomon and Lenny were unarmed.

Like wraiths in the night, they zeroed in on the tracker's location.

A dilapidated old barn stood amongst a copse of trees, it's large double doors slightly ajar. Judging from the state of the wood and paint, the barn had been abandoned many years before.

'They will have parked the Winnebago in there,' whispered Solomon to his men. 'Good cover, hidden from sight. We'll go in the front door. Move fast. Try to get hold of Reece Griffin. As long as we have him then we have some control over Brenner. There's no way he would ever endanger his friend. Lenny, as soon as we breach the doors you go for Brenner. Don't hold back. If you break him, he'll heal. Ready?'

Howard nodded but Lenny let out a low moan and held his hands to his head.

'What seems to be the problem, meatloaf?' asked Solomon.

'Head hurts. A lot.'

'So?'

Lenny grunted. 'So, nothing. Just hurts all the time. Getting worser and worser.'

'Listen, big man,' said Solomon. 'You're no good to me if you're going to mope around all day clutching at your head. Understand?'

Lenny nodded and stood a little straighter, although the pain was still etched across his face.

'Good,' continued the man in black. 'Now, let's go get them.'

They sprinted for the doors, Solomon holding himself back so as not to totally outdistance the other two men.

Then they entered the barn together.

Solomon's night vision picked it up straight away.

The barn was empty.

No Winnebago.

No Reece Griffin.

And no sergeant Ded Brenner.

Instead, in the middle of the barn stood a small cairn of stones. And on the top, the tracker, and a note.

The note was dated the day after Griffin had purchased the Winnebago. Solomon picked it up and read it.

Dear Weasel, it said. *Just how stupid do you think I am? Fuck you very much, your old buddy, Griff.*

PS. When this is over you and I are going to have a serious talk about etiquette.

Solomon threw his head back and laughed.

Griff pulled the Winnebago into the parking area outside the bar. Harleys, beat up pickups, and a Mack truck.

Brenner raised an eyebrow.

'What?' asked Griff.

'Nothing,' answered the big man. 'I was just wondering why we always stop at these sorts of places when we want to get some grub. Why never a Cheese Cake Factory or an Olive Garden or Red Lobster?'

'Really?' retorted Griff. 'You wanna stop at a Cheese Cake Factory?'

'No,' admitted Brenner. 'Not really. As I said, was just wondering.'

'Because we would stand out like dog's balls in a place like the Olive Garden, here we're as close to invisible as possible. We blend right in. Also, these sorta places don't care if you order beer at ten in the morning, and most of them don't give a shit if you smoke. Red Lobster, jeez, give me a break.'

'Just a question, Griff.'

'Yeah, just a stupid question. Come on, let's get some beer and chili.'

The two friends entered the building, stood for a couple of seconds to let their eyes adjust to the gloom, then sat at the bar.

'Couple of Buds and two plates of chili,' said Griff.

'Don't got chili,' noted the barman as he served up two bottles of Bud.

'What you got?'

'Sloppy Joes.'

'And?'

'And nothing. You want?'

'Yeah,' answered Griff. 'Give us four. And another two beers.'

The bartender slammed two more bottles down then went through to the back. Emerging mere seconds later with two full plates. Four Sloppy Joes, the mince piled high on the buns. Next to each, a ragged piece of lettuce and a tired slice of tomato. The establishment's nod toward salad.

He placed them on the bar, added a bottle of pepper sauce, knives and forks, and a pile of cheap paper table napkins.

Brenner and Griff ate wordlessly for a while. The Joes were under-seasoned and dry, but the beer was wet, and the juke box hammered out Buffalo Springfield and The Doors. Altogether, it was an acceptable atmosphere.

Brenner finished eating first. He took out a pack of Lucky Strikes and gestured to the barman. The barman nodded and slid an ashtray over, backing up Griff's theory that these were the kind of places that eschewed the smoking ban.

The big man was about to light up when the hairs on the back of his neck stood up. With the snap of his fingers both cigarettes and lighter were back in his pockets and he was standing, surveying the room.

Griff stopped eating and stood next to him.

'Wassup, big dude?' he asked.

'Something's going down,' answered Brenner.

'What?'

'Not sure. But it's got to do with us and it's not good. Look at these people.'

Griff glanced around the bar. No one was specifically looking at them, but he could sense a tension. Like the whole place was wound up real tight, ready to spring into action. Like an aircraft just before a jump. Something was definitely wrong.

Then Brenner moved, leaping the bar in one swift motion. A shotgun thundered, and plaster fell from the ceiling above Griff's head as Brenner ripped the weapon from the barman's hands, reversed it and smacked it into the side of his head. The sound of wood striking bone crunched across the room and Griff heard the barman hit the floor.

At the same time, it seemed like everyone in the bar moved at once. Weapons were drawn, people stood, and chaos was unleashed.

Griff vaulted over the bar just in time to avoid a flurry of shots from the rest of the customers.

'What the fuck is going on?' he shouted at Brenner.

'No idea,' answered the big man as he handed the pump-action shotgun to Griff. 'But it seems like we both just got mighty unpopular here. Everyone's trying to kill us.'

The firing stuttered to a halt then a man called out. 'Hey. Throw the shotgun out here as well as any other weapons you got, and step out with your hands in the air.'

'Why y'all shooting at us?' asked Griff.

'As if you didn't know,' replied the man.

'Well that didn't throw much light on the situation,' whispered Brenner.

'If we throw our weapons out, will you let us leave?' shouted Griff.

'Don't be stupid,' answered the man. 'But the reward is dead or alive. It's up to you which state you wanna be in.'

'What reward?' asked Griff.

'You got ten seconds. Then we start shooting again. Your choice.'

'I have no idea what's going on,' admitted Griff to Brenner. 'Mayhap you better sort this out.'

'I thought you said we would blend in here,' said Brenner. 'No Red Lobster because we'd stand out like dog's balls. Tell you something, buddy, if we were at an Olive Garden right now there wouldn't be thirty plus gun wielding patrons trying to off us.'

'Times up,' shouted the man.

'Sure is,' agreed Brenner as he exploded into Wolfman form and smashed his way straight through the bar, not even bothering to jump over.

'Show off,' called out Griff as he took shelter behind the remnants of the shattered furniture. He kept the shotgun ready but didn't trouble himself to look at what was going on in the room. He had every confidence Brennerwolf would take care of things. Instead, he lit a cigarette, lay back and listened to Hendrix on the juke box, the song almost loud enough to drown out the sounds of breaking bones, gunshots and screams of agony.

After less than a minute, the song stopped. As did the noises of battle.

'Hey, you coming?' growled Brennerwolf.

Griff stood, dropping the shotgun as he did so. 'Sure. Songs over anyway. Let's go.'

The two friends picked their way through the carnage and headed back to the Winnebago.

'I see you didn't keep anyone for questioning,' noted Griff.

'Sorry.'

'No worries. Just would have made things easier.'

They climbed into the RV and continued heading east.

CHAPTER TWENTY-SEVEN

Brenner drove while Griff surfed the net, looking for reasons as to why they had just been attacked by a room full of strangers.

'This is not good,' said the old man.

'Define, not good.'

'Looks like some big hitter has put a price on our heads. Must be the oil dudes.'

'How much?'

'Five big ones.'

'Five hundred thousand?'

'No,' answered Griff. 'Five million.'

'Shit,' cursed Brenner. 'I'm tempted to hand myself in for that much. But jokes aside,' continued the big man. 'We're in big shit. No wonder those dudes in the bar went for us. We're not gonna find many friendly faces between here and San Antonio.'

'It gets worse,' said Griff.

'How?'

'Well, from what I can pick up on the dark net, it looks as through the same dude has put out some sort of corporate contract on us as well. He's offered companies the five million plus all documented expenses.'

'What's that mean?'

'It means,' answered Griff. 'That every professional hit man, mercenary group and outside contracting firm is gonna be coming for us.

Probably a good deal of officials as well, cops, military, government. Five million buys a lot of hunting and grunting, plus the fact they get their costs back, means no expense will be spared. We'll be lucky if the fucking Home Guard doesn't come to the party.'

'True,' admitted Brenner. 'That is worse. What now?'

'To be honest,' answered Griff. 'No idea. Keep driving. I'll keep thinking. Eyes peeled for an ambush and let's take things as they come.'

Half an hour later they entered the Navajo Nation reservation. A massive area of land covering almost thirty thousand square miles. And with a population of around one hundred and seventy-five thousand, that meant much of the land was empty.

'Why the roads so crappy?' grumbled Brenner after twenty minutes of driving through drifts and potholes.

'They're not all bad,' answered Griff. 'I suppose there's no real reason to blacktop them all. Most of these roads probably only see a couple of vehicles a week.'

Brenner stared out of the windscreen for a while, eyes crinkled up against the sun. 'Man,' he said. 'There is literally nothing out there. Where does everybody live?'

'Holbrook, Show Low, Winslow. Five, maybe ten thousand people in each city. There's definitely a lot of nothing here.'

'Except for that,' said Brenner, pointing down the road.

Griff squinted against the light. 'What is it?'

'Person walking,' answered Brenner. 'Looks like an old lady. Strange, I didn't see her before and this has been a dead straight road with line of sight for the last twenty minutes.'

'Also, where's she come from?' asked Griff. 'And where the hell is she going to? I mean, we're like fifty miles from everywhere.'

'How am I supposed to know,' said Brenner. 'Let's ask her when we pick her up.'

Griff nodded as Brenner brought the Winnebago to a halt.

Brenner had been correct. It was an old lady. Stooped and gray, she carried nothing but a walking stick or, more correctly, a staff. It was slightly taller than her, plain carved and worn smooth with age.

She wasn't even carrying water.

Brenner jumped out of the Winnebago and approached the old woman.

'Grandmother,' he greeted her. 'May we offer you a lift?'

She turned to face the big man and raised an eyebrow. 'You're late,' she scolded.

Brenner did a slight double take. 'Umm … sorry?'

'Never mind, as we Navajo say, you must take the big potato with the little potato.'

'I thought that was an Irish saying,' countered Brenner.

'Rubbish,' snapped the old woman. 'Where do you think the Irish got their potatoes? From us. Now help me up.'

Brenner took her hand and helped her up the steps into the RV, noting as he did so she wasn't nearly as frail as she appeared.

'*Yá'át'ééh*, Grandmother,' said Griff.

The old lady snorted. Who's your grandmother, old man,' she asked.

Griff laughed. 'It's a sign of respect,' he said. 'Not belittlement.'

'So,' she continued. 'You speak the proper language?'

'*Bééhózin da*. A little,' admitted Griff.

'Where are you going?' asked Brenner

'Who said I am going anywhere?' retorted the old lady. 'Perhaps I have already arrived. You assume because I have left one place I am heading for someplace else.'

Brenner stared in silence for a while, then he shook his head and turned to Griff. 'Hey, dude. Shits going down again.'

'What the hell do you mean?'

'I mean, this sorta crap has been happening to me long enough I know when something weird is about to happen. Okay, Grandmother,' continued the big man. 'Spit it out. What's the problem?

'Hey, watch your tone, young cub. I will be treated with the respect due or I will knock the wolf right out of you.'

'So,' retorted Brenner. 'You know I'm a wolf. No big surprise there.'

'Obviously,' asserted the old woman. 'It's as plain as the broken nose on your ugly face.'

'He doesn't like ugly,' interjected Griff. 'Prefers, ruggedly handsome.'

The old woman laughed. A sound like and old car struggling to start. 'In his dreams.'

Brenner folded his arms and scowled.

The old woman winked at him. 'How about you offer me a cigarette and we talk some?' she said.

Brenner took out a pack of Lucky Strike, knocked three out and handed them around. Griff sat at the table opposite the old woman and Brenner lit them all up.

'Talk to us, Grandmother,' said Brenner after he had taken a deep drag on his cancer stick. 'Who are you? I suspect you have been waiting for us. How long, and how did you know we were coming?'

The old woman nodded. 'My name is Yiska. It means, the night that has passed. I am what my people call, *diyin nihookáá' ya haine'ii*. Loosely translated I suppose you might say, prophet or seer. But in actuality I am more akin to a receiver. A receptor of knowledge imparted by the spirits of the Holy People. The Changing Woman, the Spider Woman, and the Talking God.

'They told me you would come, but the timing was indistinct. So, for the last two months I have wandered this stretch of road. Walking there and back again. Waiting.'

Yiska took a drag of her cigarette, burning it right to the filter, then she waved it at Brenner. The big man took the butt and used it to light the old woman a fresh cigarette that he handed to her. She nodded her thanks.

'And now you have arrived,' she continued. 'The *Ataa Annaa.*'

'The who, what?' asked Brenner.

'*Ataa Annaa.* War father?' ventured Griff.

'Close,' conceded Yiska. 'That would be the literal translation. But to us it translates more correctly as, the Protector.'

'Okay, cool,' said Brenner. 'For simplicity's sakes, I'll accept I am the Protector. For now. What do you want me to do?'

'What do you know about uranium mining in the Navajo Nation?'

Both Griff and Brenner shook their heads.

'Not much,' admitted Griff. 'I know large amounts of uranium were discovered here. That's about all.'

'Okay,' said Yiska. 'It's a long story, but I'll cut it as short as I can. Large uranium deposits were found on the reservation back in the nineteen thirties. No one really cared until the cold war began and nuclear proliferation started. At that time, the United States Atomic Energy Commission declared it was the sole legal purchaser of uranium in the United States. It then contracted private mining companies for the product.

Needless to say, none of these companies were Navajo owned. The Nation simply didn't have the money or expertise at the time to get involved with such things.

Private companies then hired many Navajo employees to work the mines. Disregarding the known health risks of exposure to uranium, the private companies and the United States Atomic Energy Commission failed to inform the Navajo workers about the dangers and to regulate the mining to minimize contamination. As more data was collected, they were slow to take appropriate action for the workers. Studies show the Navajo mine workers and numerous families on the reservation have suffered high rates of lung disease, cancers, and other diseases, from environmental contamination. For decades, industry and the government failed to regulate or improve conditions, or inform workers of the dangers.

'Finally, after proving the Navajo that had worked on the mines were up to two hundred times more likely to contract various forms of cancer than the average population, the mines were closed. That was in two thousand five after literally thousands of deaths from exposure. And still, even now, cancer cases continue to rise because of how deeply the uranium extraction has affected the water, the air, and the ground. In fact, there are still over a thousand open uranium mines that need to be cleaned up.'

Brenner scowled. 'I love my country,' he said. 'But there are times when I am truly disgusted by what we have allowed to happen to our own people.'

Griff nodded his agreement. 'A sad story. But there is little we can do about historical injustice, Grandmother.'

'I know that,' snapped Yiska. 'I'm old, not senile.'

She pointed at Brenner's pack of Lucky Strikes and the big man lit up another cigarette and passed it over.

'There is still a demand for uranium,' continued Yiska. 'And contrary to popular belief, uranium is not that expensive. It's not like precious metals. So, the best way to maximize profit is to cut costs to nothing.'

'I think I can see where this is going,' said Brenner.

'A mob of so-called businessmen have reopened some of the old uranium mines,' confirmed Yiska. 'They are taking our young men and forcing them, at gunpoint, to labor there. There is no ventilation, no safety protocols and no regard for human life. To be taken by this group of thugs is to be issued with a death sentence.'

'What about the cops?' asked Griff.

'We have a small police force,' admitted Yiska. 'But not only are they overworked; they are also not keen to take on superior forces. You see, we are not a wealthy people, and with poverty comes fear of not being able to support one's family, or indeed to even retain one's job.'

'What are you talking about?' asked Griff. 'Bribery or blackmail?'

'Both. They are scared of losing their jobs. And to be brutally honest, we have had problems with corruption. But even more than that, it is simply a lack of will to stand against the *status quo*. We are a proud nation, but we have suffered terribly under the draconian laws and subjugations of white America. As a result, some of us have given up.'

Brenner nodded his understanding. 'I get it,' he said. 'So then, Grandmother, how can we help?'

'Hey, Ded,' interrupted Griff. 'Sorry, friend, but before you mount up and start charging at windmills, don't forget we're pretty stacked up here. You remember, what with the oil companies trying to off us, places to go, people to kill, sort of thing.'

'People are suffering,' stated Brenner. 'And we are here.'

There was a pause for a while as no one spoke.

Eventually Griff said. 'That's it? That's your pithy argument? We're here.'

The big man grinned. 'Is there any other reason?'

Griff shook his head. 'No. I suppose not. Who else but us?'

'It's settled then,' said Yiska. 'Come, take me to my hogan. You can meet some of my people while you plan your campaign.'

'Fine,' agreed Brenner. 'What's a hogan?'

'Traditional Navajo dwelling,' replied the old woman.

'Cool. Let's go,' said Brenner with a grin.

Griff fired up the Winnebago and they headed north.

CHAPTER TWENTY-EIGHT

Yiska's harjo was situated on a flat area of dirt surrounded by a few scrubby trees. To the right a patch of corn. Maybe ten rows. On the left, a double- wide trailer. At the back, a toilet, an open shower, and a small water tower.

Standing outside the double-wide was an old man and a young girl. The man was patently not of Navajo ancestry. The girl was.

Griff parked the RV and they helped Yiska alight.

The old lady hugged the girl then stood next to the man. 'This is Duncan Shirley,' she said. 'My man. And this here is Doli. She is my acolyte. A shaman in training. Already very powerful. Headstrong. This here is Griff and Brenner.'

Duncan shook both of their hands.

Doli nodded and smiled. Then she bowed to Brenner and greeted him. '*Yá'át'ééh Ma'litsoh.*'

Yiska turned to the big man. 'She said …'

Brenner waved his hand in dismissal. 'I know. Something like, welcome Wolfman or, hi there, barking boy.'

Yiska nodded.

'Yep,' said Brenner. 'I see where this whole thing is going. Used to be that I could keep my affliction a secret, but now everyone knows what I am.' He bowed to the girl. 'Greetings to you, Doli, acolyte and shaman to be.'

Doli grinned and grabbed Brenner's hand. 'Come,' she said as she led him to the trailer. 'We got soda. And a fridge, so it's real cold.'

The group trooped into the trailer and Doli ushered them to the sitting area. Bench sofas, built in, foam cushioning with faded floral coverings in mustard yellow and orange. In the middle of the room a Formica table. The same orange color.

'What soda you want?' asked Doli.

'What you got?' asked Brenner.

'Big Red and Big Blue.'

The big man raised an eyebrow. 'You choose.'

Doli opened the small fridge and hauled out five cans. Two red and three blue. She handed one of the blue ones to Brenner. He popped it open, saluted all and took a sip. It tasted of corn syrup and water. But the little girl was correct about the temperature. It was ice cold.

'Yiska foretold you would come,' said Duncan. 'I believed. But after a few weeks I did begin to lose a little faith.'

'We're here,' noted Brenner.

'So, you going to save those poor boys?' asked Duncan.

'Mayhap,' answered Brenner. 'First we gotta have a plan. How many are there, and where are they? That would be a good start.'

Both Yiska and Duncan turned to Doli.

'She is the one who has been in communication,' said Yiska. 'You will need to ask her. But remember, she is young, and her power is still unformed, so her visions may lack clarity.'

Brenner nodded. 'Okay, Doli. Tell me what you know.'

'They come to me in my sleep,' she started. 'But they can't talk, only show. They are sad. Most have no mothers or fathers. They sleep in different houses or in old buildings. The bad men find them and take them to work the mines. The work is very hard and very dangerous. Many die. They are locked up when they aren't down the mines. They come to me at night. They cannot talk but their spirits cry out. They need protection. They need help. They need *Ataa Annaa.*'

'Where are they?' asked Brenner.

Doli shook her head. 'In a bad place.'

'East? West? Any idea?' continued the big man.

Again, Doli shook her head.

'I can find out where they are,' said Yiska. 'Tonight, I will dream walk with her. I will recognize the place. I have been alive so long I know this land well.'

'Cool,' said Brenner. 'Why didn't you do that before?'

'It will put a huge strain on Doli,' answered the shaman. 'I wanted to wait for your arrival before I risked the girl.'

'Maybe we shouldn't do it then,' said Brenner. 'We can find another way. A way without risk to Doli.'

Yiska shook her head. 'No. She is acolyte. She is shaman. It is her duty and her place. Tonight, we walk together. Tomorrow we know.'

Northwest,' said Yiska. 'Past Tuba City and on toward Bitter Creek. There is a place called *Asta Dzil*, or Eagle Mountain. It has no eagles, nor is it in any way a mountain, so I know not why it is named so. But I do know it is a place of bad magic. A poisoned land. There is an abandoned mine there. That is where you will find them.'

'How many?' asked Griff.

'More than twenty. Less than thirty,' answered Yiska.

'Guards?'

The old lady shrugged. 'Yes. I couldn't see how many. They had large guns.'

'Shotguns?' asked Brenner.

Yiska shook her head. 'I don't know much about weapons, but they looked military. They had curved magazines. Like bananas.'

'Brenner cursed under his breath. 'AKs. I bloody hate assault rifles.'

'There won't be that many guards,' ventured Griff. 'Doesn't take that many to keep control of twenty to thirty youngsters. Depends if they're working two or three shifts, but I reckon twelve to fifteen. At least a third sleeping at any one time.'

'Fifteen men with AK 47s,' quipped Brenner.

'What's this sudden obsession with assault rifles?' asked Griff.

The big man shrugged. 'Just hate getting shot, I suppose. Hurts.'

'Well don't get shot, then.'

'I always get shot.'

'True,' admitted Griff. 'Anyway, we gonna need some sort of transport. I can't fit that many people in the Winnebago. Any suggestions?'

'School bus,' said Duncan. 'I drive the local school bus, but the kids are on holiday, so we can use it.'

'Nice one,' said Griff. 'Well, no time like the present. Let's tool up and head out.'

'I'll drive,' said Duncan. 'The bus is a temperamental old bitch and the gearbox needs nursing.'

'Doli and I will also come,' stated Yiska. 'I trust you will keep us safe.'

'Can't make any guarantees,' said Brenner. 'But we'll do our best.'

***

It had taken them longer than they planned to reach the mine. The last three hours they had crawled along what Yiska had insisted was a track, but Griff referred to as virgin ground. Two miles before their destination Yiska called a stop. Brenner and Griff tooled up and proceeded on foot.

Griff carried an AR15 and two extra magazines. Brenner carried his rucksack with an extra set of clothing. They both wore khaki shirts and trousers that blended in with the surrounding landscape like desert camo. So, as long as they didn't allow themselves to be silhouetted against the skyline, or raise any dust from their footsteps, they were nigh on invisible as they moved swiftly and carefully toward their target.

After ten minutes Griff raised his hand. 'Stop,' he whispered as he lowered himself to the ground.

Brenner went down beside him, scanning the surrounds. 'What? Have you seen someone?' he whispered back.

Griff shook his head. 'No. I'm just beat.'

'Why?'

Griff stared at the big man. 'Why? Seriously? Because I'm getting close to eighty fucking years old. I have arthritis, I smoke like a Frenchman, and drink like an Australian. I take ten minutes to piss in the mornings and I can hardly see any more.'

Brenner didn't say anything for a while as he thought. Then he spoke. 'Bullshit. Your eyesight is fine.'

Griff shrugged. 'True. But I'm going for the sympathy vote here, so I thought I better pile it on. Whatever, I need a break. Do us no good if I'm all in when we get there. I may not be going hand-to-hand, but I still need to provide overwatch.'

'I could carry you if you want.'

Griff sneered. 'Piss off. I'm old, not an invalid. Tell you what, why don't you go wolf and we can strap a saddle to you, then I can ride you.'

Brenner laughed. 'Okay, point taken. Rest. Tell me when you're ready to rumble.'

A few minutes later Griff stood. 'Let's go.'

Brenner nodded and took the lead. Still moving fast but at a lesser pace than before.

They breasted a small hill and the mine came into view. A row of tattered tents. Five of them. Behind the tents a large prefab building. Outside the building a large generator. The prefab boasted three window-mounted air-conditioning units, and Brenner guessed it was the guards' dormitory.

Rolls of rusted razor wire ringed the area, and six guards patrolled the interior in pairs. All carrying AKM assault rifles.

'Wonder how many guards inside the mine?' asked Brenner.

'No idea,' admitted Griff. 'I would guess the bare minimum. Maybe none. If it were me, then I would rather stay out in the fresh air than spend any time down a radioactive mine with no safety features. Reckon the rest of them will be crashing out in the air-conditioned hut.'

'How is your line of sight?' asked Brenner.

'Good enough. I can cover you from here. How do you want to play it?'

'I reckon I go full wolf,' answered Brenner. 'Creep up as close as. When I get about twenty yards away you open up on them. Try to take at least a couple down. Then I'll jump the wire and finish them off. If any come running from the building or the mine, take them out. After I have finished with the outside guards then I'll move into the building. I'll try to keep at least one alive, find out who's in charge of this concentration camp. That seem workable?'

'Fine,' said Griff. 'And when we've sorted the guard problem out?'

'I'll go human. Dress and go into the mines. You come down as well. Check for wounded, clear weapons, and make sure no one leaves.'

'Let's do it.'

Brenner nodded, stripped down and changed.

Wolf.

Moving like a shadow he slid across the landscape. Almost invisible, even when you knew exactly where to look. Griff's eyes watered as he concentrated on the huge supernatural being.

Brennerwolf stopped moving and lay down some twenty yards from the rolled razor wire. As he did so, Griff raised his AR15 to his shoulder, sighted on the pair of guards closest to Brenner, and squeezed the trigger.

The sharp crack of the 5.56mm round rent the desert air and the first sentry went down, a puff of dust exploding from his shirt pocket. Griff tracked right and squeezed the trigger again. Once, twice. Man down.

He moved again, picking up the next pair of guards who were running toward the downed men. The AR15 barked again and one of the guards went down in a flurry of arms and legs. The second, knelt and started to return fire, but his AKM was set to full auto and the shots screamed impotently over Griff's head as the rifle's recoil sent the barrel skywards.

Then Brennerwolf entered the fray.

Assault rifles chatted insanely. Lead flew, and blood flowed.

Brennerwolf entered the hut.

Two guards appeared from behind the hut and Griff cut them down with a hail of metal. Then he sprang to his feet and jogged down to the gate. It wasn't locked so he simply kicked it open and ran over to the doorway of the prefab building.

When he got there Brennerwolf was exiting, morphing back into human form as he did so.

'Two probably still alive,' said the big man as he started to put his clothes on and headed toward the mine.

Griff ventured into the prefab, his rifle at high port. Ready.

Inside there were dead guards and pieces of dead guards. There was no one left alive. Not even close. Griff sighed loudly. But he didn't blame the big man. He knew, when Brenner went full wolf there was no holding back. The animal saw an enemy and it destroyed an enemy. There were no half measures.

Ten minutes later the big man called from outside.

Griff walked out to see around thirty young men. They all looked to be in appalling shape. Starved to emaciation, dehydrated, filthy and covered in minor cuts and abrasions. He took out his cell phone and rang Duncan. 'It's done,' he said. 'Bring the bus.'

'Anyone we can question?' asked Brenner, gesturing toward the prefab.

Griff shook his head. 'Unless you got a Ouija board.'

'Sorry,' apologized Brenner.

'No worries,' said Griff. 'We just ask the dude in charge of this lot what he knows.'

'There's no one in charge,' countered Brenner. 'Just a bunch of exhausted prisoners.'

Griff shook his head. 'There's always someone in charge. Or, there is always someone that thinks he's in charge. Amounts to the same thing. They normally know what's going on.'

'Okay,' said Brenner. He walked to the fringe of the crowd. 'Hey,' he yelled. 'Who's in charge here?'

A small wiry man walked over. 'Me,' he said. 'My name is Motega.'

'Told you so,' said Griff.

Brenner grinned, but before he could ask any questions the yellow school bus rattled into the compound and Duncan, Yiska, and Doli jumped out.

They greeted everyone then headed for the prefab.

'We're going to look for water and medical supplies,' said Yiska.

Brenner held his hand out. 'Not Doli,' he said. 'Some of the guards were in there.'

The old lady nodded and told Doli to wait outside.

Moments later Yiska and Duncan reappeared carrying adequate supplies of food that they portioned out to the ex-prisoners. Then they helped to dress wounds with the scant medical supplies they had found. Mainly plasters and antiseptic cream.

After their administrations, the young men still looked broken but were no longer at death's door.

Duncan wandered over to join Griff, Brenner, and Motega.

'Good work,' said Griff to Duncan. 'Now, Motega, a few questions. Actually, only one real simple question. Who is in charge of this mining set up?'

'Oh, that's easy,' replied the young Navajo. 'It's Derek Chee. We ain't never seen him but the guards talk. They all proper scared of him. Yeah, Derek Chee be the man.'

Griff smiled. 'Well, that was easy.' He looked at Brenner. 'Now, we find this Chee dude, explain nicely to him and go on our way. No problemo.'

The big man nudged Griff and pointed at Duncan.

Duncan had gone as pale as a shroud and looked like he was having trouble breathing.

'Hey,' said Griff. 'You okay? What's up. Are you having a heart attack or something?'

Duncan shook his head. 'Man,' he said, his voice little more than a whisper. 'We are so fucked. So absolutely, utterly, and completely fucked.'

Yiska walked over from the bus. 'Come on, gentlemen,' she called. 'Let's get moving.' Then she too looked at Duncan. 'Are you alright?' she asked with concern as she rushed over and grasped his arm.

Duncan shook his head again. 'This mining set up,' he said. 'It's being run by Derek Chee.'

Yiska swayed slightly, even though she was holding on to Duncan's arm. 'But why?' she asked no one in general. 'Surely he has enough money without doing this sort of thing.'

'No,' denied Duncan. 'It's not about the money. He is true evil. It is about control. Leverage. The people that uranium will give him access to. Whatever, it no longer matters. Nothing matters. Before the week is out, we will all be dead.'

'Hold on,' said Brenner. 'What's with all the doom and gloom? Just who is this Chee dude, and why the long faces?'

Duncan took a deep breath. 'Derek Chee is looking to be the next CEO of the Navajo Nation Gaming Enterprise. The man is a gazillionaire. Owns shopping malls, RV parks, construction. You name it. And he is as shady as fuck. Incredibly dangerous. Apparently, he has no enemies. Not one. Living that is.'

Brenner shrugged. 'So? Bigger they are, harder they fall, and all the usual clichés.'

'No,' interjected Yiska. 'Chee is no normal man. He is an adept at dark magik. He is a skinwalker.'

'This skinwalker thing,' said Brenner. 'Means he can turn into an animal. Isn't that what I am?'

Yiska sucked in a sharp intake of breath. 'No,' she said firmly. 'Very different. He is a human adopting the guise of an animal through dark magik, by stealing the animal's soul. You, on the other hand, are a wolf that has become human for a while in order to help. Big difference.'

Brenner decided that his whole, failed army experiment thing should stay under wraps for a while, rather than muddy the already murky waters. 'Anyway,' he said. 'How will he even know it was us who rescued his prisoners? There's no surveillance there.'

Yiska raised an eyebrow. 'What, you not been listening, wolf boy? I already told you, Chee be big on magik. He knows. Trust me.'

'Okay,' said Griff. So, he's coming for us. Big deal. Any idea what sort of fire power the man is gonna bring?'

Duncan shrugged. 'I don't know. Lots.'

'Guess. And try to be a little more accurate than lots.'

'I can only go by rumors,' continued Duncan. 'But people say he has at least two hundred armed men under his control. Also, lightly armored vehicles, rocket launchers, access to outside contractors. Maybe more.'

Griff lit a cigarette. Breathed out. 'He's right you know,' he said to Brenner. 'We are like, so fucked.'

Brenner nodded. 'Yeah. Man, even for us those are big odds.'

'So, what do we do?' asked Griff.

Brenner laughed. 'We ignore the odds and go kick this dude's ass, big time. It's a fucking moral imperative. And anyway, Surrender is not a ranger word.'

'Rangers lead the way,' added Griff.

CHAPTER THIRTY

Brenner and Griff found Derek Chee at one of his casinos. In all fairness, he was an easy man to find, making no secret of where he was at any time. In fact, he reveled in his notoriety. Surrounded by a bigger entourage than a rap star and more women than Hugh Heffner, he cut a swath through his surrounds like a meteor through midnight space.

A large man, he radiated an animal magnetism that was hard to ignore. Teeth as white as innocence, maroon Western style suit, and alligator skin cowboy boots. On his head the traditional head band, tied in a knot at the back.

'Looks like a super-douche,' commented Griff under his breath.

'Nice boots,' said Brenner, as they both watched the man sashay his way across the casino floor, patting backs, shaking hands, schmoozing, and socializing with all. His general heading appeared to be taking him toward the exit.

Brenner and Griff followed.

Chee left the casino and climbed into a civilian Hummer, followed by three burly men and three women. It was obvious from the solid sound when his driver closed the door, the Hummer had been upgraded regarding its armor.

The vehicle pulled out of the parking lot followed closely by another two Hummers that held the rest of the entourage. Griff waited until they were far ahead before he pulled out and followed.

After a couple of miles, the three Hummers pulled off the main road. Griff donned a pair of night-vision goggles and cut his lights before he took the same turning, ensuring there was no chance they could be seen.

Around five miles later the convoy of large vehicles stopped. They were at a building site. The skeleton of a multi-story building reared up against the night sky. Floodlights lit the area, casting long shadows that cut across the strips of white light.

Griff coasted to a halt then he and Brenner alighted, closing the doors softly behind them.

They moved closer to the entourage, stopping a few yards outside the pool of light cast by the floodlights.

Griff carried his AR15 and two extra magazines.

Brenner carried nothing.

The two friends lay still under the cover of darkness as they watched. Brenner strained his super sensitive hearing to listen in.

'What gives?' whispered Griff.

'The dude is seriously blowing his own horn,' answered Brenner. 'Apparently, this is the site of his newest casino. He's telling everyone how he built his whole empire up from nothing, he's the king, bow down before me, blah, blah. The usual self-absorbed bullshit you'd expect from this sort of douchebag.'

'Should I just shoot him?' asked Griff.

'Can you hit him from here?'

Griff sneered. 'Really. Barn door, dude. Can't miss.'

Brenner nodded. 'Well, it's what we're here for. A little anticlimactic, but what the hell. Take him out.'

Griff raised the rifle to his shoulder, slipped the safety off, sighted and took a slow breath.

But as he concentrated on Chee, the man turned and looked directly at him.

Then he started to change.

Unlike Brenner's graceful metamorphosis from human to more than human, Chee's transmutation was a thing of violence and horror. The flesh seemed to melt from his face as a ragged maw grew in its place. Claws punched through the ends of his fingers, and bones snapped and reformed. Blood and ichor flowed freely as the beast emerged, head thrown back, jaw agape, as it screamed in agony.

And in the place of the man known as Derek Chee stood a monstrous mountain lion.

It was immediately obvious from the reactions of the entourage that some had seen the change before. Mainly the men. Others, the women on the whole, had not.

Females in evening gowns screamed in terror, running in circles or simply fainting where they stood. All the men drew weapons and started to fire in Griff and Brenner's direction.

Griff returned fire. However, the harsh glare of the lights and the movement of the antagonists made targeting near impossible. But still, some of his shots struck home, bringing the reward of bright red blood and sharp cries of pain.

The mountain lion roared, its voice ringing across the desert like a call to arms. A challenge.

Then Brenner began to run. As he moved, he flowed from his human form into the Wolfman hybrid. Muscles shifted effortlessly to reveal the supernatural. Clothes burst and scattered as he grew in size. Claws and teeth extended smoothly, like swords being drawn from silken scabbards.

And Brennerwolf howled his acceptance of the challenge.

Atavistic and primal it shattered the very air itself. This was no mountain lion. No modern remnant of what once was. This was the original predator. The Alpha of all alphas.

The very acme of the food chain.

This was … the Wolfman.

The supernaturals met under the ring of floodlights, crashing together like two opposing weather systems.

Chee fought like a wild animal. A demented beast. All claws and teeth, and spitting and yowling. A force of nature.

Brenner fought like an army ranger with over fifty years of combat experience … in the form of a massive predator.

Even Chee's closest friends would not have called it a competition.

Within seconds, the dismembered body of Derek Chee, entrepreneur, gangster, skinwalker, and child kidnapper, lay scattered across the building lot. The mountain lion reverting to its human form as it expired.

But far from losing heart, Chee's men increased their efforts to hit back. All weapons were brought to bear on Brenner and, seconds later, the sound of a helicopter could be heard, hammering across the desert toward them.

Discretion being the better part of valor for the time being, Brennerwolf decided to run, picking up Griff and throwing him over his shoulder as he did so.

The old man didn't argue as the two of them disappeared into the night, moving at a little over seventy miles an hour. Three times faster than a top Olympic sprinter.

As soon as they got to the Winnebago, Griff donned his night goggles and they took off at best possible speed, lights off, heading away from any possible pursuit.

They drove in silence for just under an hour, directionless, simply moving. Then Griff stopped next to a small copse of scrubby trees. He turned off the engine and sat for a few seconds.

'Okay,' he said. 'What the fuck was that?'

'Some type of mountain lion,' answered Brenner. 'Big one.'

'How?'

Brenner shrugged. 'Don't know. Never come across that sorta thing before. Always reckoned the whole skinwalker legend was rumor. Figured I was the only thing like that around.'

'Well, you can't say that anymore,' snapped Griff. 'Holy shit. What if there are more of them?'

'No problem,' said Brenner. 'They're not that tough. Stupid as well. Like animals. I reckon he had a false sense of his worth. Probably every time he changed, people just crapped themselves and didn't even bother to fight back.'

'That's not really what I meant,' said Griff. 'I mean, well, you're not alone.'

'I wasn't alone before,' said Brenner. 'And just because some Navajo had some weird power makes no difference. I am what I am, and he is, was, what he was. End of story. Now let's try to get some shut eye. I reckon tomorrow might end up being a little stressful.'

***

Two hours later Brenner shook Griff awake.

'Wassup?' muttered the old man. 'Morning already?'

Brenner shook his head. 'An hour and a bit until sunrise. But listen.'

Griff sat up. 'Helicopter?'

'No,' said Brenner. 'Three helicopters. As far as I can tell. They're doing an aerial grid search. They also appear to be coordinating with ground troops. I've been out there watching. It looks like the Navajo dudes. Not military. Seems like Duncan was correct. They gonna chase us like forever. It's an honor thing.'

'So?' asked Griff.

'So, we run some more,' answered Brenner. 'There's helicopters and at least a hundred plus guns on the ground. Let's get moving. We'll head toward San Antonio. That's where Taylor the oil dude is, and it's as good a direction as any. Come on, lets saddle up.'

Pieter Leroux had been a Kommandant in the South African army. A rank similar to a Lieutenant Colonel in the United States military. He had left the SADF after the transition from apartheid to full democracy, and he had joined an outfit called Executive Solutions. Ostensibly a South African-run mercenary army sponsored by American money, and used throughout the world to further American interests.

And now he and his men were out to get Brenner.

He had gathered thirty of his very best men in three E-Series Ford, fifteen-seater RV's. Unlike the usual civilian people movers, these were lightly armored vehicles with run-flat tires and upgraded suspension. And instead of fifteen, each carried ten men plus full combat gear.

Personally, Pieter thought it was total overkill. Mister Taylor had told him the target consisted of two old men and a dog in a Winnebago. Pieter would have dispatched one E-Series at most to deal with such a low-level threat.

But Taylor was paying the bills as well as promising a multimillion-dollar bonus, so three full teams he got.

To be honest, this looked like it would prove to be the easiest money he had made this year. Taylor had seemingly endless access to surveillance and people on the ground, and it didn't take long to track down the Winnebago in question. The day before it had been seen entering the Navajo Nation Reserve heading from the west toward the east.

Then they had lost sight of them. But it didn't take a genius to work out they were most likely heading for San Antonio to complete whatever strange vendetta they had against mister Taylor and his people.

So, Pieter had simply driven into the Nation Reservation and formed an ambush on the single main road that would provide the Winnebago access to the route to San Antonio. He blocked the road with one of the Fords then placed the other two on the flanks. The ambush itself was situated as the road took a sharp bend around a large hill so as they came around the mountain they would literally be almost on top of the ambush.

He placed a lookout on the hill and waited.

He would then spring the trap as soon as they came into range and simply shoot the living crap out of the Winnebago.

After all, the reward stated dead or alive, and dead was so much easier.

***

'Must go faster,' shouted Brenner.

'Shut up,' said Griff. 'Instead of giving useless advice why don't you take a few shots at them. Try to slow them down?'

'You're joking, man. There's like two hundred of them. Must be forty vehicles and two helicopters at least. Can't you use that caltrop device? Scatter some spikes on the road?'

'I already did that two miles back,' answered Griff. 'Why do you think three cars suddenly flipped over?'

Brenner grabbed an AR15, leaned out of the window and pulled off a few rounds. The answering fire was deafening as steel-jacketed rounds hit the Winnebago, starring the back windscreen and pockmarking the bodywork.

'Well that didn't work very well,' shouted Griff. 'Maybe we'll lose them around this bend.'

'Wishful thinking,' said Brenner.

'Hey, don't knock it. It's all we got left.'

Pieter Leroux's two-way radio crackled to life and he pressed the receive button. 'Go for Kommandant,' he said.

'Sir, It's corporal Wynand here. Lookout on the hill.'

'What is it, Corporal? Our target in sight?'

'Yes and no, sir.'

'Which is it, Corporal. Can't be both.'

'Target is in sight,' affirmed the corporal. 'But it's not just a single Winnebago, sir.'

'So, our old men have picked up some reinforcements,' said Leroux, a hint of amusement in his voice. 'How many?'

'Hundreds, sir.'

'Say again, Corporal.'

'Hundreds, sir. All armed. Coming at us full speed. Holy shit. They're opening up. I am returning fire.'

The sound of gunfire echoed plainly across the landscape as the Winnebago came careering around the mountain, spearheading what looked like a convoy of forty to fifty vehicles.

'Open fire,' screamed Leroux. 'Everyone, open fire.'

A cacophony of weapons chattered to life, raking the convoy with machine gun fire.

And the convoy fired back.

***

'Who the hell are these people?' shouted Griff. 'What the fuck is going on? Why is everybody shooting everybody else?'

'I have no idea,' answered Brenner as he primed the M202A1 FLAME rocket launcher Dave had given them. 'But I'm all for creating a little extra confusion.'

He leaned out of the window, aimed the weapon at the convoy behind them and pulled the trigger. Then he swiveled smoothly and fired at the ambush in front of them.

The two napalm filled rockets sped through the air, trailing plumes of white smoke behind them. Then they detonated almost simultaneously.

The result was beyond spectacular.

Huge swathes of greasy orange flame billowed skywards like an airborne napalm strike. Vehicles exploded, burning men screamed in agony, and hundreds of rounds of ammunition cooked off, filling the superheated air with the vicious buzz and whine of supersonic lead.

'Holy shit,' exclaimed Griff. 'Way to go.'

Brenner pointed at a rough track that lay at right angles to the road. 'Go down there,' he said. 'Let's get the hell out of Dodge before these fuckers stop fighting each other and concentrate on us.'

Needing no extra encouragement, Griff slammed his foot to the floor and sent the RV bouncing and jolting down the track at top speed.

CHAPTER THIRTY-THREE

Pieter Leroux surveyed the aftermath around him, his head in his hands, his expression slack with disbelief.

Oily black smoke marked the area like a massive funeral pyre. Men lay dead and dying around him. The attacking convoy was retreating, their remaining vehicles disappearing around the mountain.

It had been a close-run thing, being outnumbered at least six or seven to one, then the napalm strike. It was only the experience and the discipline of his men that had not only kept them from being over-run, but also helped beat the enemy back.

However, the worst of it was that while they were busy trying to survive, the Winnebago with the two old men and the dog had escaped.

He took out his cell phone and dialed a number.

It was answered on the first ring.

'Pieter,' greeted the voice. 'Talk to me of good news.'

Leroux didn't speak for a few seconds, instead, controlling his breathing.

In. Out. In. Out.

Like it was no longer an autonomous act.

Then he said.

'Mister Taylor?'

'Yes.'

'Mister Taylor,' he said again. 'Fuck you very much, you son of a bitch.'

'Watch your tone of voice, boy,' answered Taylor. 'Just you remember who you are talking to.'

'Fuck you once more, asshole,' retorted Leroux. 'I have lost twelve of my men. Good men. Men I have known for my whole life. And by the end of the day, I will lose more. Burned to death.'

'I don't understand,' said Taylor. 'What the hell are you talking about?'

'What am I talking about? You SOB. Two old men and a dog, you said.'

'Wolf,' snapped Taylor. 'I said, wolf.'

'Whatever. What you didn't say is they would have backup. Forty vehicles. Two hundred armed men. Helicopters. They had fucking air support. They hit us with napalm. You never mentioned that, did you?'

Neither man spoke for a while.

'I am truly sorry,' said Taylor, eventually. 'I honestly have no idea how this happened. As far as all the intel went, they were a renegade pair of old men. Ex-Vietnam nuts. Obviously, we've got the whole thing wrong. Look, Pieter, your company will be compensated. Your men will be compensated. And their families. You have my word.'

'Good,' snapped Leroux. 'Because if they aren't, then you have my word, mister bloody Taylor. I will come to see you, and I will tear you a new asshole, you incompetent son of a whore. I swear it on my dead friends' graves.'

Leroux cut the connection.

And hundreds of miles away, Brandon Taylor dropped his cell phone from his shaking hand and screamed for his head of security.

'Tony. Get in here now, we have a problem.'

Johnny Adakai was the second in charge of 'Five Card Holdings', and on Derek Chee's death he had been granted full leadership.

The first thing he had done was to lead the attack on the two men who had assassinated their ex-boss. It was an honor-bound duty, and all had followed him without question.

Now, however, after their disastrous defeat, there were mumblings of dissent.

The top twenty board members had gathered in the Fowler Suite, named after golfer Rickie Fowler whose grandmother was Navajo. It was a magnificent room, boasting enough space to comfortably seat the score of men and their bodyguards.

Situated on the top floor, some twelve stories up and accessed by a single guarded elevator it was both sumptuous and practical.

A long balcony with its open, plate glass sliding doors afforded a unique view of the surrounding landscape below, the half-moon shining off the desert sand and turning into a sheet of blue velvet.

Unlike a normal American corporate meeting of the board, teamed with soft plump men with hard minds, manicures and entitlement, this board was made up of men who had fought their way up. Physical men with hands like leather, and faces scoured by the outdoors. Men who were hard in both body and deed. Men who simply didn't take crap from no one.

And they were not happy.

'Listen, Johnny,' said headman Tom Tso. 'There's no way around this. Today's escapade was a disaster. We lost forty good men, ten vehicles and a fucking helicopter. And the blame must fall on you. As you know, it is our way. The buck stops at the top.'

'Tom,' replied Johnny. 'How was I supposed to know those two men were leading us into an ambush? We had no idea they were part of a larger group. Even now we have no idea who we are fighting. None of us do, and I know for a fact you have all spent the entire day trying to find out.'

Tom raised an eyebrow in acknowledgement. It was true. Their entire network of intelligence had brought up nothing. No one had an inkling as to who had declared war against 'Five Card Holdings'.

'And regardless of today's losses,' continued Johnny Adakai. 'We are still bound to avenge Derek Chee's death. And we will still be bound to do so even until the last one of us dies trying. You know that this is true.'

There was a general ripple of agreement as the board mumbled their consent.

'So, this is what I say,' said Johnny, taking advantage of the prevailing feelings. 'We gather our strength. Then we put all effort into finding these men and killing them. Nothing else matters. It is our duty and we are honor bound. They must die. Are we all in agreement?'

'Sorry, old chap. Afraid not. You see, Brenner is strictly off limits.'

Every head in the room turned toward the voice.

The stranger stood on the balcony. He was of medium height and build, dressed all in black that contrasted diametrically with the death-like pallor of his skin. He exuded a confidence and a sense of self-assurance that was literally palpable. An almost physical force.

'Who the … how did you get there?' asked Johnny Adakai. 'Who are you? And what the hell are you doing here?'

'So many questions,' said the man in black. 'How did I get here? Not important. Who am I? My name is Solomon Hopewell. And what the hell am I doing here?'

The man smiled. And the overhead lights reflected off his two large, razor-sharp canines. There was a collective gasp from the men in the room.

'Well, I'm here to stop you bringing any harm to Ded Brenner. Colonel's orders, you see. Normally I would have sent Lenny. New assistant of mine. Large chap. Dumb as a bag of hammers, but a physically impressive creature nonetheless. However, he seems to be suffering from debilitating headaches of late, so I've given him the evening off.' The man sighed. 'Needs must and all that. I'm sure you all sympathize.'

Adakai shook his head in disbelief. 'Good God, will someone please shoot this long-toothed motherfucker so we can continue our meeting.'

One of the bodyguards drew his pistol.

There was a clap of sound as Solomon moved so quickly, he defied sight. A soft expulsion of air. The sound of blood pattering onto the plush carpet like autumn rain and the dull sound of a body hitting the floor.

And now Solomon was standing on the other side of the room.

As one, every man drew his weapon and opened up on the man in black. Slugs ricocheted off marble pillars, men dropped from friendly fire, windows shattered, and the air filled with smoke and screams.

Something smashed into Johnny Adakai. He felt both of his legs break as he fell to the floor, such was the power of the hit.

Twenty seconds later all was still.

The man in black stood over Johnny, his expression one of slight boredom. He wasn't even breathing hard.

'What are you?' grunted Johnny.

'You know, old chap,' he answered. 'I am no longer really sure how to answer that. Bit of a crisis of identity at the moment. I suppose you could say I am the thing that goes bump in the night. The shadow at the end of the corridor. The monster under the bed.'

Johnny nodded. 'I get it, my worst nightmare.'

The man in black raised an eyebrow. 'No,' he said. 'Not at all. That would be Brenner. I doubt I even come close.'

'Could have fooled me.'

Solomon nodded. 'Yes, given your current predicament, I can see how the subtleties would be lost on you. Fair enough.'

'What now?' asked Adakai.

Solomon walked over to one of the chairs that were dotted about the room. Copies of Louis the Fifteenth furniture. Solid oak and gold brocade. Heavy. He picked one up in his left hand, then tore the one leg off with his right. Like a glutton ripping off a chicken drumstick.

Swinging it back and forth a couple of times he got its measure.

Then he walked back to Adakai and stood over him, the leg raised high.

'Shit,' said Johnny.

'Yes,' agreed Solomon.

CHAPTER THIRTY-FIVE

They had made it. They charged into the valley of death and came out of the other side relatively unscathed.

Griff had been driving with a purpose for the last two hours and Brenner hadn't spoken, allowing the old man to give his full attention to their escape.

Now the sun was a couple of hours from setting and they were out of the Navajo Nation Reserve.

Alive.

Elated, Brenner turned to Griff to congratulate him. But as he did so, the old man slid from his seat and the Winnebago drifted slowly to the side of the road and stalled.

With frantic but careful movements, Brenner picked Griff up and carried him through to the bunk at the back of the RV. Then he lay him down and quickly searched his body for any wounds. Cuts, gunshot, or other.

Nothing.

But the old man was as pale as death. Lips a pastel blue. Breathing shallow and pulse slow, weak and erratic.

Brenner moved him into the recovery position, consulted the SatNav then headed for the nearest town as fast as. Foot pressed firmly to the floor.

***

Brenner wondered when they had started letting twelve-year old's become doctors. The physician facing him made Doogie Howser look like an octogenarian.

'You father is responding well to treatment,' he informed the big man.

Brenner said nothing to dispel the youngster's belief in Griff's parental status, knowing it would be easier for the hospital to believe they were related.

'What's wrong with him?' asked Brenner.

'As far as we can tell, nothing in particular. He simply seems to be suffering from extreme exhaustion. He's dehydrated, lacking in nutrients and there doesn't seem to be an inch of his body that isn't displaying a bruise, abrasion, or recently healed wound of some sort. Quite frankly, mister … I'm sorry, I didn't get your name.'

Brenner nodded his agreement. 'No, you didn't. Carry on.'

The doctor sniffed in disapproval but continued his assessment. 'Quite frankly, sir, if your father was a minor, we would have called social services. He's an old man and you should be taking better care of him.'

Brenner looked suitably chastened as the doctor's words sank in. 'You're right, doc,' he admitted. 'I've been a bad … son. Can I talk to him?'

'For a short while only. He's on a drip and he's under sedation. He needs rest. We shall keep him here for overnight observation. If he ticks all the boxes tomorrow, then we will discharge him back into your care.'

'Thank you.'

The doctor gestured for the big man to follow, and he led him to a small private room. Single bed. Cream walls. Yellow drapes. A single light-wood table and the standard battalion of machines that went beep and hiss. The cheap severity of the room belying the fact it was costing Brenner over six times more than a top five-star hotel for the night.

Griff looked up and scowled as the two men entered the room.

'Hi, Dad,' greeted Brenner with a grin. 'Good to see you looking a little better.'

'Dad yourself, you fucking idiot,' grunted Griff. 'Where the hell am I? What happened? Didn't get shot, did I?'

'Of cause not, Dad,' continued Brenner with a warning look. 'Why would you have been shot. We were just driving down the highway and you passed out.'

Griff glared at Brenner, then he nodded at the doctor. 'Who's the kid in the lab coat?'

'I'm Doctor Soames.'

'Fuck off,' quipped Griff. 'Does your mommy know you're not at kindergarten?'

'Come on, Dad,' said Brenner. 'The young doc has done a great job. Now we'll leave you to get some rest. I'll be back tomorrow, okay.'

'You call me dad again and I'll stick this drip so far up your ass it'll scrape your brain loose.'

Brenner shook his head. 'Sorry, Doc,' he apologized. 'Old people can be so rude. I apologize on behalf of my father.'

The doctor went over to Griff's drip and injected a small syringe of clear liquid into it. Seconds later, Griff's eyelids drooped, and he fell asleep.

Then the doctor turned to Brenner. 'Look, sir,' he said. 'I'm not an idiot. When two men who look like the pair of you come into my hospital with no form of identification, and proceed to pay for treatment with large wads of used bills, I know better than to ask too many questions. As to the case of this man being your father? Well, friend, maybe, but let's not push too hard, shall we, I may look young, but I wasn't actually born yesterday. Suffice to say, I know trouble when I see it. I just want you both out of my hospital before whatever crap you're in follows you here. Now please leave and I shall see you here to-morrow, mid-morning. Copy.'

Brenner nodded. 'Copy, Doc. And thanks.'

CHAPTER THIRTY-SIX

I don't understand,' said Howard.

'Which words?' asked Solomon. 'Pray, tell me and I shall explain each and every one of them to you.'

The driver flinched very slightly. He had worked with the man in black for many years now and he knew him well. His facial expressions, his moods, and his capabilities.

And when he looked like he did right now, people tended to die. Badly.

'Sorry, sir,' said Howard. 'I misspoke. I'll set course and proceed back to the farm with all haste.'

'Do so,' said Solomon. 'And don't call me sir. I'm still a sergeant, Corporal Howard. I work for a living.'

And the man in black cradled Lenny's head in his lap as he pushed a stray lock of hair from his forehead. 'Don't you worry, meatloaf,' he whispered. 'Sergeant Solomon is going to get you all fixed up. We're going to see the healing lady. She'll make things better.'

So, Howard drove back toward the town of Pepperpot. Then beyond. Seeking chief Kohana Harjo, and doctor Materia Santiago.

The lady who had turned Solomon's black eyes blue.

The healer.

CHAPTER THIRTY-SEVEN

Rather than drive into Dave's prepper cave, Brenner parked the Winnebago outside and waited.

There were a few reasons for this, the main ones being, he wasn't sure if Dave had boobytrapped the entrance and, secondly, he wasn't sure who would be there to greet him if he simply drove in. Dave Cornell, or his eminently more dangerous and flakier alter-ego, Thaddeus Meriwether Cornell.

So, he sat back, lit a cigarette and did nothing un-toward. Halfway through his Lucky Strike he saw a movement out of the corner of his eye as Dave rose out of a small copse of shrubs twenty yards from the RV.

Brenner had known he was there, having spotted him when he first lit up. But he was still impressed at the man's ability to move almost undetected through the landscape. And the big man was also sure that anyone without his innate wolf-heightened senses wouldn't have picked up the prepper.

Dave walked up, and Brenner got out of the Win-nebago to greet him.

'Dave.'

'Brenner. What gives?'

'I brought Griff back here for a bit of R & R. Hope you don't mind.'

'Of course not,' answered Dave. 'He been shot?'

Brenner shook his head. 'Simply worn out. Been pushing himself too hard. Taken a few hits, lack of sleep, dehydrated. Generally, all fucked-up.'

'He hates to admit he's getting older,' said Dave. 'Is he awake?'

Brenner shook his head.

'Well, drive in and we'll get him to a room when he wakes.'

Brenner drove the RV into the cave and they left Griff in the bunk. Then he followed Dave inside. As he entered the room, he heard running feet and a body launched itself at him like a kamikaze pilot.

'Brenner.'

'Hey, Cloe. How goes?'

'Fine. Dave has been teaching me how to track. Animals and people. Also, how to shoot, field strip my weapons, fight with a knife, make a fire without using matches, hunt for food. I even ate some bugs, they were yukky. Tasted like vinegar. Dave says even though they taste like shit, you can live off them if you have to.'

'Language,' mumbled Brenner, but Cloe was too excited to hear, and she kept up her one-sided conversation all the way through to the kitchen where the big man helped himself to a jug of water and sat.

After a few minutes, James pitched up and greeted the big man, albeit in a slightly less effusive fashion.

Dave started to cook up a late lunch. Chicken fried steak, bacon, and corn bread.

Brenner noted the complete lack of vegetarian options but didn't say anything.

As Dave placed a large platter of meat on the table, together with knives and forks, Griff walked into the kitchen.

Cloe greeted the old man with the same enthusiasm as she had greeted Brenner, almost knocking him off his feet before he recovered.

He sat and stared grumpily at everyone.

'What are we doing here?' he asked.

'R & R,' answered Brenner as he helped himself to a heaping pile of steak and bread.

'Don't need no rest and recuperation,' snapped Griff. 'I'm all recuperated already. Just needed a good night's sleep.'

'Yeah,' agreed Brenner sarcastically. 'And an isotonic drip, B vitamins, magnesium, hydrocortisone, sedative. The list goes on.'

'Whatever. I'm all better now.'

'Better than you were,' admitted Brenner. 'But look, my friend. You were lights out for a while there. Running on empty. So, I reckon you stay here for a short while, provide eyes and ears for me via the web and whatever other ways you can, target acquisition, info. Everything like that. Meanwhile, I'll be the feet on the ground. I'll take out whoever needs taking out. Sound good?'

Griff looked at his friend like he had just slapped him. 'You're benching me?'

'Resting you,' denied Brenner.

'I can take it, Ded,' insisted Griff. 'Don't put me out to pasture, man. I'll push harder. I can do better. Please don't treat me like some invalided old man. Please.'

Waves of guilt threatened to swamp the big man. He knew how much Griff hated getting older. How much he denied it. And how well he did at the sharp end, despite his advancing age. But the fact of the matter was, the pace was too swift, and it was only a matter of time before Griff either collapsed completely or, worse, got shot and killed. And Brenner wasn't sure he would be able to live with the death of his only friend on his conscience.

He shook his head. 'From now on, I work alone.'

Griff stood and limped off, turning to Brenner just before he walked through the door. 'Fine,' he said. 'Fuck you, you selfish prick. Do what you want.'

The rest of the meal was finished in awkward silence. There was nothing much to say.

When Brenner was finished eating, he stood. 'I'm doing the right thing,' he said to everyone.

They all nodded. But no one spoke.

***

Brenner loaded the long length of chain into his saddlebag together with the padlock. He heard someone approaching, but when he looked up he was disappointed to see it wasn't Griff.

He was about to greet Dave when he noticed he was wearing a monocle and his hair was loose.

'Thaddeus?' he greeted with the slight nuance of question.

'Of course,' returned Thaddeus with a frown. 'Who else?'

'Sorry,' apologized Brenner. 'Got a lot on my mind.'

'He's merely upset,' said Thaddeus. 'Not so much with you, as with life. The seeming unfairness of mortality is getting to him. Particularly when he sees his old compatriot staying eternally youthful *ala* Dorian Gray.'

Brenner pointed at the chain. 'Swings and round-abouts.'

'I understand,' said Thaddeus. 'And I feel the strain you are under. Rest assured you are doing the right thing. For now. But you must also realize something else. There will come a time when a warrior would rather die with his boots on than wither away in a bed or at a desk.'

Brenner nodded. 'I get it. I am not my brother's keeper. It's just that he looked so frail. Man, I thought I'd lost him. I don't know what I would have done if I had.'

'Get used to the idea,' said Thaddeus. 'Not to put too harsh a light on it but, lose him you will. Lose everyone, over time, you will. You may very well have to face the fact it is not your lot in life to gather companions. It is simply your lot to fight the good fight.'

'Yeah,' agreed Brenner. 'I've thought about that before. Obviously.'

'It would have been remiss of you not to have.'

'It sucks,' said Brenner. 'But what can you do?'

Thaddeus laughed and thumped the big man on the back. 'Stiff upper lip and all that, my good man,' he said. 'Remember, the blows that do not kill us make us stronger. It's always darkest before the dawn, and any other such manner of hideously inappropriate clichés.'

Brenner straddled his bike. But just before he started it, he heard a shout.

'Hey, wolf boy. You leaving without saying good-bye?' Griff walked up and put his hand on the big man's shoulder. 'You take care, Ded,' he said. 'And don't forget to check in via the sat phone. Remember, I got your back.'

Brenner smiled. 'Thanks, Griff. I'll keep in touch. Shouldn't take me that long.'

The two friends looked at each other for a few seconds before Griff put a fake stern look on his face. 'Right then,' he said. 'Off with you. Places to go and people to kill. Move on.'

Brenner nodded, flicked the starter, gunned the engine and thundered away.

Both Griff and Thaddeus watched him fade into the distance.

'How long have you known him?' asked Thaddeus.

'Forever,' answered Griff. 'Met him in 'Nam. Sent the two of us on a deep incursion mission. Real under the wire stuff. Gather information, avoid the enemy at all costs. Stay frosty and stay out of sight.'

'He was good?'

Griff chuckled. 'He was fucking useless.'

Thaddeus raised an eyebrow in surprise.

Griff noted his expression and laughed. 'Hey, don't get me wrong. The man was a machine. Jungle craft second to none. Cool as a cucumber, hard as a lump hammer. But he just couldn't listen to orders. We went in, uncovered a forward base and saw there was a Russian colonel there. An "advisor". They had an American pilot. Were torturing the poor bastard. Heavy stuff. What we should have done is take pictures. Map the place out and leave. Let the brass take care of it. Not Brenner. Next thing I knew, he'd sneaked in, iced the Russian and the guards, taken the pilot and killed everyone else on the way out.

Unbelievable demonstration of skill. He was twenty years old at the time. Same as me.

'When we got back, technically he should have been in the shit, but the pilot was some politicians son-in-law so Brenner got a medal instead.'

Griff shook his head. 'After that, if anyone needed killing, they'd call the team of Griff and Brenner. Fuck knows why they thought I was part of it. I was just a spectator, man. Someone who stood on the sidelines while this force of nature wreaked death and destruction on thine enemies. There were times he scared me. But I love the SOB, truly I do.'

'And he, you,' said Thaddeus. 'But you're right, there's something primal about Brenner. But he is a reactive force, not a proactive one, which is lucky.'

'Not sure I understand,' admitted Griff.

'He does not seek out trouble,' said Thaddeus. 'Although he rails against injustice and impropriety, he does not seek it out. But if it presents itself then he attacks it with furious anger. I say that is lucky, because imagine a man of his power actually seeking to become involved. Looking for trouble. Taking it upon himself to police the general public. It's almost as if ...'

'What?'

Thaddeus shook his head. 'Ridiculous theory. But it's almost as though Brenner has been chosen for his role in life. Chosen by a higher being. He doesn't need to look for trouble, because he is steered in the right direction by this higher being, this overlord. Like a questing knight. Or a guardian angel. Silly, really. The musings of an irrational man.'

'No,' disagreed Griff, as he thought of the Watchers. The two mysterious old men who watched over

Brenner. And the indisputable fact that trouble always found Brenner, never the other way around. 'It's not as farfetched as you may think. Not at all.'

And Thaddeus smiled.

CHAPTER THIRTY-EIGHT

The sky was still blood red, but to all intents and purposes the sun had gone below the horizon.

Solomon waited for Howard to open his door then he stepped out of the luxury limousine.

Lenny followed, his movements slow and uncoordinated. He clutched at his head as he walked.

Standing in a group around the car were at least twenty people. All were well armed. Shotguns, assault rifles, and pistols.

In the van stood chief Kohana Harjo and, to his left, the Healer, Materia Santiago.

'You are not welcome here, dark man,' said chief Harjo.

'And yet here I am,' stated Solomon. 'And do please put those weapons down. We all know that with, or without them you are all helpless. I could kill the lot of you before you get a single shot off. Well maybe a single shot.' Solomon turned to face Matty. 'You. I need your help.'

The healer shook her head. 'Never.'

Solomon continued as if she hadn't spoken. 'Good. It's Lenny, you see. Silly chap has developed a case of debilitating headaches. Can hardly function at all anymore. He tells me there's nothing that can be done about them. Says the fellows back at the Project said this would happen. Now, he's of no use to me if he can't perform at peak, so I thought you could help. If not, well, probably have to have the poor thing put down, obviously.'

Matty stared at the man in black for a few seconds. 'You care,' she said.

Solomon shrugged. 'I do, or I don't. It is of no matter. Can you help him?'

'I see your eyes are still blue,' continued Matty. 'Strange that. Any corresponding changes? Like caring about your colleagues?' she smirked.

'Stranger things have happened,' admitted Solomon. 'But whatever, it hasn't changed the fact I cannot abide time wasters. And you, dear healer, are starting to waste my time. Will you help, or would you rather I go postal on this little enclave of yours and you can see how well you can deal with healing mass dismemberment.'

'I will help him,' said Matty. 'But not because of your threats. I'll help because he needs help.'

Solomon waved his hand in the air. 'Yes, I'm sure. My threats are meaningless, I help where help is needed, blah, blah. Still wasting my time. Do it, or don't do it and suffer the consequences.'

Matty held out her hand to Lenny. 'Come,' she said. 'Let's go and sit under cover from the sun and I'll take a look at you.'

Solomon started to follow but Matty shook her head. 'Not you,' she said. 'You stay here. Or go somewhere else, I don't care. But not with us.'

Solomon nodded. Unconcerned. Then he simply went and sat in the back of the limousine with the aircon on full.

Matty led Lenny to chief Harjo's Winnebago and seated him in the covered area outside. The huge man dwarfed the chair he sat in and it was obvious he was in pain, but struggling to not show it.

'Would you like some cold water?' asked Matty.

Lenny shook his head.

'Okay then,' continued the healer. 'You just sit there and try to relax. All I am going to do is place my hands on your head for a while. You might feel a bit strange when I do so. Dizzy. A bit disoriented and maybe even nauseous. Don't worry. It's totally normal. Is that alright with you?'

Lenny nodded. 'My head hurts,' he whispered. 'Like it's on fire.'

Matty walked behind the man mountain, placed her hands on his head, took a breath and concentrated.

Twenty minutes later she staggered to her chair and sat. Her hair was lank and drenched with sweat. Her shirt likewise. Her face, pale and bloodless. She breathed like she had just run a four-hundred-meter sprint.

And her eyes were filled with unshed tears.

'Are you alright, ma'am?' asked Lenny.

Matty nodded. Took a sip of water. 'Lenny,' she said. 'Why are you hunting Brenner? What has he done wrong?'

Lenny looked stunned. 'He never done nothing wrong, ma'am,' he said with conviction. 'He's an American hero. It's just that he's strayed. The colonel says Brenner is important to the country and he needs to come back home. That's why we look for him. We don't want to hurt him or nothing. We just want him to come back to us.'

'Solomon wants to hurt him.'

Lenny shook his head. 'No. Not really. But the sergeant don't know how to do things without hurting. It's what he does. He's not a bad man.'

Matty smiled. 'He is a bad man, Lenny. A very bad man. And I think he hates Brenner.'

'No way, ma'am,' insisted Lenny. 'He don't hate Brenner. He afraid of Brenner. He reckons, mister Brenner be the most powerful thing around. Maybe the most powerful thing on the planet. It's just Brenner don't know it yet. But if we can bring Brenner home then the colonel can teach him how to find his true power.'

'What power?' asked Matty. 'What does the colonel, whoever he is, say about Brenner?'

'The colonel is the head of the project,' said Lenny. 'And as to what he says about Brenner, he say, "And his judge shall be the evening wolf, and he shall leave nothing till the morning". That be from the bible, ma'am.'

'And what does the colonel mean by that?'

Lenny shrugged. 'I don't rightly know, ma'am. I know Brenner be the wolf. That's all.'

'And his judge shall be the evening wolf, and he shall leave nothing till the morning. Her prophets are light and treacherous persons: her priests have polluted the sanctuary, they have done violence to the law. The just Lord is in the midst thereof; he will not do iniquity: every morning doth he bring his judgment to light, he faileth not; but the unjust knoweth no shame.' Matty swung around to see Solomon standing there. 'Scripture,' he said. 'Zephaniah 3.3 to 3.5.'

'I don't get it,' admitted Matty. 'Why does he say that?'

Solomon smiled. A humorless grimace. 'The colonel's got a real hard-on for Brenner. He's always quoting biblical shit about him. No idea why. All I know is Brenner has never been officially dismissed from the United States Army, and as such he is still the property thereof. Hence, we need him to come back, and until then he is absent without leave. A fugitive on the run. That is all you need to know. Now, have you cured Lenny?'

Matty gestured with her head then walked away from the man mountain. 'You sit there a while,' she said to him. 'Sergeant Solomon and I are going to have a chat.'

Lenny nodded and stayed in the chair, hands between his legs, back hunched. A four-hundred-pound child.

Matty led Solomon around to the back of the Winnebago and, as they were out of sight, she launched a massive slap at the man in black. Although she had moved quickly and had given no warning, Solomon swayed effortlessly out of the way. Then he raised an eyebrow.

'Sorry,' he said. 'Pure reaction. If you'd like to take another swing I won't move. I know how frustrating it is to try to hit someone and miss. Actually, I don't, but I can imagine.'

'You utter bastard,' hissed Matty. 'He's a child. You monster. To do that to a little boy. How can you live with yourself?'

'I live with myself fine,' answered Solomon. 'Now, what the hell are you rabbiting on about? I know Lenny's a bit slow, but he's not a child. Just dumb as a box of horseshoes.'

'He was seven years old when you lot got hold of him. He's twenty-one now. For the last fourteen years he's been locked up in a room, experimented on, beaten, shocked, filled with drugs. Punished for any transgressions. Torture, Sergeant. Plain and simple. Torture.'

Solomon frowned. 'Look,' he said. 'I must admit, I had no idea. I simply assumed the big man was an adult when they took him in. But, whatever. Needs must and all. What the colonel does at the project is for the good of the nation. War is won by those who are willing to sacrifice the most. And we are those people. The ones who are willing to sacrifice to protect our way of life.'

'Oh, fuck you,' shouted Matty. 'What does a seven-year-old boy know about sacrifice. I saw his memories. He knew nothing. He was taken from an orphanage because of his genetic makeup. His specific blood type. And from that day on he knew only different levels of pain.'

'Sometimes sacrifice is forced upon us,' muttered Solomon. But Matty could see he wasn't convinced. 'Anyway, thanks for curing him, I owe you one. We have work to do.'

'I haven't cured him,' snapped Matty. 'I've managed to relieve the pain for a while. That's all.'

'What do you mean?'

'I mean he can't be cured. Whatever you and your precious colonel did is killing him. He has a tumor the size of a baseball in his head. The pain was so acute I am amazed he could even breathe. But he's still dying. The damage was far too great to stop. I may have given him some extra time. That is all.'

'How long?'

'Worried if you have enough time to complete your mission, sergeant?'

'How long?' repeated Solomon.

Matty shrugged. 'A few more days without debilitating pain. Of life … who knows? Days, definitely. Weeks, maybe. But not months.'

Solomon said nothing.

'Are you alright?' asked Matty.

Solomon grinned, exposing his fangs. 'Sure. Why wouldn't I be? I mean, I work alone at any rate. Already told the colonel that.'

And turned around and walked off.

But not before Matty saw the pain on his face. The expression of loss.

'Hey, dumb boy,' he shouted at Lenny as he walked by. 'Come on, stop lounging about on army time. The healer says you're cured. Now let's go. Move it.'

The man mountain stood and lumbered after the man in black. Master and servant. Private and sergeant.

Friends?

Both Kohana and Matty watched them leave, the limousine kicking up a plume of dust as it spun away at high revs.

'Unfeeling animal,' said Kohana vehemently.

'Maybe,' said Matty. 'Maybe. But his eyes are still blue.'

Kohana raised his eyebrows in question. But Matty added nothing to her thoughts.

Then she smiled.

CHAPTER THIRTY-NINE

The Harley thundered through the night. A dark horse. On it, a man bent on vengeance. Retribution on an iron steed.

Brenner decided to travel only at night, using backroads and byways. Once again substituting stealth for speed. In the day he slept rough. The first in an old dilapidated barn. The second, hidden under a camouflaged tarpaulin. He knew the enemy he faced were all-seeing. Satellites. Men on the ground. Eyes everywhere.

And in such a case, the darkness was his ally.

He had no real plan past, find the men in charge, and do what needed to be done. He knew his primary target was in San Antonio, so he assumed whoever else was integrally involved would also be there or close enough.

He was relying on Griff to provide his intel. Until then, get close and stay frosty.

On the third night he was riding hard and the heavens opened. Rain sheeted in like a tsunami but, in the distance, he saw a red and blue neon sign, smeared into illegibility by the torrential downpour. However, he was sure it was a bar of some sort.

A haven from the storm.

As he got closer, he saw he had been correct. The sign read, 'Mama's Palace'. Outside, two rows of Harleys and a couple of three wheelers.

He pulled over, dismounted and went inside, standing in the entrance for a few seconds while the water poured off him. Then he headed straight for the bar and sat on a stool.

The barman nodded a greeting. 'What can I do you for?'

'Beer,' said Brenner. 'Anything American. You got food?'

The barman nodded as he slid a bottle of Millers. 'Sure. BBQ. Just took off a brisket. It's real good.'

'I'll take a couple of big helpings,' said Brenner. 'And some bread and another beer.'

'Sure.'

The food arrived in minutes. The plate heaped high with slices of perfect, pink brisket and, on the side a pile of burnt ends. This was followed by a plate of corn bread, a dish of butter, and another beer.

Brenner ate in silence, eyes on his food.

He was halfway through his meal when his hackles stood. Someone was looking at him. More than one someone. The big man looked around but, as he caught people's gazes they looked away.

There was no animosity. Merely curiosity. And he knew, straight away, he had been made. It was then he noticed that pretty much everyone in the bar was wearing the same patch on their jackets. 'Red Sun M.C.'

'Shit,' he mumbled to himself. 'Brenner, you are one stupid mother. Talk about staying undercover. You walked right into this one.'

As Brenner berated himself, a man stood, walked over and sat on the barstool next to him.

Neither spoke for a while. Brenner continued eating, his attention only peripherally on the man sitting next to him. He registered he was large, six three or so. Two hundred fifty pounds plus. A beard straight out of the ZZ Top catalogue. Denims, checked shirt. Leather jacket with Red Sun patch.

It was obvious from his demeanor he was the leader of the club. His poise, ease of stance and relaxed expression told all. Then he spoke.

'You know there's a bounty on your head?'

'Brenner nodded. What was the use in denial. 'Yeah. Apparently so.'

'Five million,' the man continued.

'So, you dudes going to try to claim it?' asked Brenner.

'Do I look suicidal?' asked the man with a grin.

'You got a lot of boys,' Brenner pointed out.

'Yeah,' agreed the man. 'And that's a damn site better than having a lot of body bags.'

Brenner signaled to the barman. 'Beer.' He turned to the newcomer. 'You?'

'Jack and coke'

Brenner held out his hand. 'Brenner.'

'Jackson. President of Red Sun. We've heard of you. The lone rider. Black Harley rat bike. Heard your name was Dead. Heard that if you cross the lone rider, you find yourself in a world of hurt.'

'Might do.'

'Also heard the lone rider is a straight shooter. Deals a fair hand and sticks it to the man.'

'Could be true.'

'Well, a man like that shouldn't have a price on his head,' stated Jackson. 'No sir. A man like that should be left alone to do what he does. You need any help?'

'What sort of help?' asked Brenner.

'Like a posse. We can ride with you if you want. Keep the man off your back.'

Brenner smiled. Genuinely appreciative. 'Thanks, chief,' he said. 'I ride alone.'

'Respect, dude. Tell you what, we'll get all to spread some disinformation. Report sightings of you all over the place. Ten, twenty a day. The man won't know who from what.'

Brenner stood and grasped Jackson's hand. They shook firmly, eye to eye.

Then the big man put twenty dollars on the counter and strode from the bar.

As he left, all in the room stood, their heads bowed, eyes down.

Respect. Perhaps even more. Reverence.

The lone rider

CHAPTER FORTY

Are you sure you wouldn't like it all in cash?' asked Taylor.

Pieter Leroux shook his head. 'Can't carry that much cash out of the country without raising a few eyebrows,' he answered. 'Let's just keep this all above board. The agreed lump sum for each of my men that died, and a bonus for the men that made it through the contact.'

'Fine,' conceded Taylor. 'Have it your way. The money will be in your account within minutes. Now, Pieter, a favor.'

'I'm out of favors, mister Taylor,' countered Leroux. 'They all got burned up in that napalm strike that hit my men.'

'What if the favor offered up some chance of revenge?'

'I'm listening.'

'Look, we've been getting vastly conflicting reports of where our main target is. As far away as New York to as close as Houston. Some even say he has been spotted here, in San Antonio. What do you think?'

Leroux shrugged. 'Not really my place to think, mister Taylor. I act on information given. That's my job.'

'I know, but you've been around some. Fought many battles in many different countries, give me your gut feel on the issue.'

'Gut feel?'

'Please.'

Leroux took a deep breath. 'I haven't been privileged to have been told the nitty-gritty of this whole affair. I don't even know why these boys are coming for you, but I don't really need to know that. From what I've seen so far, the things they have done, the lengths they have gone to … they're coming for you. Or at least one of them is. It's been my experience it's usually only one man you have to worry about. Out of the two men you have identified, one of them will be the killer. The man to be wary of. The other will be the side kick. You say you have had varying reports, one man or two?'

'Just the one. Single male, rides a black Harley. Big. Mean looking.'

'Which one is he?'

'Our intelligence says his name is Brenner.'

'Well, he's the one,' confirmed Leroux. 'And he won't stop until either you are dead, or he is.'

'How long?' asked Taylor.

Leroux shrugged again. 'How could I know? If it were me, I would take out the peripherals first. Chew up your allies, leave no one behind my line of attack. Then I would take you out last. Make a show of it. But who knows? He may come for you first. I'd say anything between a day to a week.'

'Can you stop him?'

Leroux thought before he answered. 'Ja. Probably. But not if he brings another two hundred people and air support like last time.'

Taylor shook his head. 'No. Although the reports of his whereabouts vary, they all agree on one thing, he is alone.'

'Well then, yes. With enough men, I can stop him,' answered Leroux.

'Do it.'

'There's a price involved,' said Leroux. 'And it's not cheap.'

'Cost is no object,' answered Taylor. 'Just do it.'

***

Three hours later, Pieter Leroux stood in the entrance to Brandon Taylor's penthouse apartment. The apartment itself was situated on the top two floors of the Associated Industries office building. A steel and glass edifice that dominated the surroundings. At forty stories and six hundred feet in height it wasn't taller than the Tower of the Americas observation platform, but it did shade the thirty-eight story Marriot Rivercenter.

And Taylor's apartment was the only residential unit in the building.

Leroux considered the place to be imminently defendable, as well as leaving room for countless ambush and choke points to gun down the assailant.

Easy money.

First, the mercenary took thirty men and split them up into six groups of five. Then he cut all power to the escalators. Next, he simply placed one in the lobby, then the next five groups on various random floors above. There was no pattern so as not to give away their potential presence.

Personally, Leroux thought his plan was massive overkill. After all, these were his best men, veterans of many wars. There was little chance this Brenner would even make it past the lobby. Let alone the killing fields that the rest of the building would become.

Finally, Leroux took his very best three men and placed them outside the doorway to Taylors apartment. He furnished them with an M2 Browning .50 caliber machine gun. Using an electric drill, his men bolted the tripod of the weapon to the floor. Then they stacked some sandbags in front of it.

Leroux pointed at the entrance door to the hallway.

'If that opens up,' he said to them. 'Then you open up. Understand?'

They nodded. 'Yes, Boss. We kill whatever comes through that door.'

Leroux nodded. 'Right. I'll be inside the apartment with the client. Take shifts sleeping. Liaise with the rest of the team. Stay alert.'

Then he went into Taylor's apartment and locked the door behind him.

The trap was set.

CHAPTER FORTY-ONE

Brenner sat up and lit a cigarette before he answered the satellite phone.

'Hey, Griff.'

'Ded, my man. How's it hanging?'

'Cool. You got news?'

'Yeah. Been tracking this main dude, Brandon Taylor that James told us about. Broken into his private coms. Looks like we got four major groups involved. Taylor, the Russians, the Chinese, and the Saudis. I'm close to getting a position on Taylor. Can't find the Russians or the Saudis, but got solid eyes on the Chinese.'

'Where are they?' asked Brenner.

'What's your position?'

Brenner told him.

'Well then they're due east of you. From what I can tell, they've rented an entire hotel. It's called 'The French Villa'. It's near an area called Paradise Canyon, some ten or twenty miles west of San Antonio. Far as I can tell there's about twenty of them. Reckon you can find the place and take them out of the equation?'

'Do turkeys hate Christmas?' returned Brenner.

'Good man. I'll keep in touch. Stay frosty.'

It was still daylight, but Brenner rolled up his camo tarp and mounted up. After he had dealt with the Chinese, Taylor would know he was coming. So, there was no use in stealth anymore. Now it was speed and brute strength.

The Harley growled to life and Brenner headed east.

***

The sun had lit the sky on fire as it sank below the horizon. Brenner watched from the adjacent hilltop. His enhanced sight meant he had no need of binoculars.

The first thing he picked up was that Griff had been correct. The Chinese had hired the entire hotel and there were in excess of twenty of them

The second thing he noticed was that there was a large ratio of servants to guests. At least ten, including chefs, chamber maids, gardeners, waiters, and reception. That complicated things. Brenner could not let them get caught up in any form of collateral damage. They were true innocents.

With that in mind he decided to wait until midnight before he made his move. Then it would be slow and stealthy.

He would become death.

CHAPTER FORTY-TWO

Zhang Wei loved America. Particularly the coffee. The gentle excess of sitting down in a diner, paying for a single cup of coffee and getting unlimited refills. He loved the cars. The music. And the high levels of customer service.

Not all his compatriots agreed. Some considered America to a be a louche society of weak, money driven individualists. People who put themselves before the general good. But Zhang Wei was honest enough to admit to himself it was natural to want things. Material goods. TVs, iPhones, fancy cars, and good clothes.

Take for example the hotel that Lin Yang, their esteemed party member and international liaison manager of PetroChina, had rented for the group. It was the ultimate in luxury. Yang could easily have chosen a less opulent establishment that would have still met all their requirements, but it was the natural order of things to take the best one could get.

Zhang Wei adjusted his shoulder holster, settling the QSZ-92 pistol into a more comfortable position as he continued to do his rounds. Of the entourage of twenty-two people that traveled with Lin Yang, only four were actual administrative staff. Of the rest, seventeen were security. Ex-military, trained for personal protection, assassination, and counter-assassination. Because in a country like China, with its

totalitarianism and its teeming population, sometimes, to protect one had to kill. And party
sanctioned murders were part and parcel of Zhang
Wei's life. As it was for all the members of the team.

The final person in any large business group traveling outside of China was always a member of the
MSS. The Chinese Ministry of State Security. And
so it was in this case. The MSS agent did not mix
with the rest of the team, instead, lurking on the pe-
ripheries, taking notes and casting dark looks. They
were always universally hated and feared at the same
time.

Zhang Wei glanced at his watch. Two minutes past
midnight. His replacement should have already arrived.

He heard Li Jie before he saw him. A large man,
he walked heavily and, at first glance, appeared
clumsy. But he was far from it, being a master of
both Wushu and Jujustu.

Li Jie rounded the corner, raised his right hand in
greeting, and disappeared.

Wei blinked then rubbed his eyes with the backs
of his hands. Jie had been there, then he wasn't. It
made no sense. The security guard drew his pistol
and walked slowly toward where he had seen Jie last.
Nothing.

Then a pool of shadow came to life.

The last thing Zhang Wei saw, was a set of ludi-
crously large teeth.

Brenner moved on, circling the building.

Through luck more than judgement, Brenner had
hit the hotel as the shifts were changing so he managed to take out twice as many guards as he would

have if he had struck earlier. Or later. A beneficial two-for-one sale.

Eight down.

It was time to enter the building.

By waiting until such a late hour, Brenner had cut the chance of collateral damage down substantially. From a bevy of servants, there was now only a night manager, a maid, and an assistant chef in the kitchen. A number he could easily work around.

He entered the hotel via an open store room door at the rear. Ghosting in on padded feet. Crouching to fit through doorways, using his hearing and sense of smell to reconnoiter ahead of him.

He came across three armed guards chatting in one of the corridors. None of them had time to draw their weapons.

He hid the bodies in a broom closet and moved on.

Another man alone in his room. Afterward, Brenner pulled the bedclothes over the corpses head and shut the door behind him.

Room to room, retribution stalked.

The plague in solid form.

Bring out your dead.

Then there was only the main suite left and, as far as Brenner could figure, only the leader still to account for.

He decided to ramp up his attack and eschew silence, so he simply kicked down the door, going for shock and awe.

The room was listed as the presidential suite and the designers had not exaggerated.

It was huge. A dining area, enough lounge furniture to seat fifteen plus people. A variety of occasional chairs and tables and, at the far end, a full wet bar.

The room was also full of people. Standing at the bar, a slightly built Chinese man, his suit expensive but still badly fitted. He was attempting to assume a debonair and unruffled expression. But the rivulets of sweat and the flushed face belied his efforts.

'Ah, yes,' he said. 'The wolfman. We have been expecting you.'

'Well you didn't do a very good job then,' growled Brenner. 'Because all your other men are dead.'

The man waved his hand dismissively. 'Meaningless. Mere grist for the mill. Now, however, you get to meet our true operatives. Say goodbye to your trivial life, mister animal person. It is time to die.'

Brenner scanned the other men in the room, registering for the first time they were all dressed in identical uniforms. Black Kung Fu outfits, soft black shoes, and black scarves wrapped around their heads, disguising their identities.

He chuckled. 'Really,' he said. 'Ninjas?'

The Chinese man at the bar shook his head. 'That is Japanese discipline,' he spat. 'These are *Lon Kuei*. The forest demons. They were flown in specially to deal with you. And they are your death.'

'No,' said Brenner. 'They're just a bunch of dudes with swords, which is, I must warn you, not a life prolonging situation to be in right now.'

Then without any further warning he attacked.

To be fair, the *Lon Kuei* were good. Fast, well trained, and agile. One of them even managed to cut Brenner on his shoulder. A deep slash that healed within seconds. But ultimately, their movements were too prescribed. A form of combat copied and passed on for hundreds of years, mired in tradition and ritual. It was no contest when pitted against Brenner's combination of animal violence and human street fighting. A vicious, unpredictable mélange of controlled fury and unbelievable physical strength.

Within seconds, the Wolfman had his hand around Lin Yang's neck.

'The Russians and the Arabs,' he said. 'Where are they?'

'Are you going to kill me?' asked Lin.

Brenner nodded.

'If I tell you, will you make it quick and clean?'

'I will.'

'They have banded together. They are on a large boat on Medina Lake.'

Brenner took Lin Yang's head off with one blow.

CHAPTER FORTY-THREE

The view of Medina Lake was magnificent. Brenner had ridden through the small town of Lakehills, stopping for a quick bite at the 4-way bar and grill. A jalapeno cheese burger that had tasted like more, so he had ordered another two and had bolted them down like a starving Rottweiler.

Now he was parked above the Medina Lake camp ground, looking out over the eighteen-mile-long, crescent-shaped reservoir.

On his way in, he had scouted much of the lake and it had become immediately apparent there was only one boat afloat on the water that would be large enough to fit the bill. A massive paddleboat called the Medina Queen.

With a twist of the throttle, Brenner rode on down to the lakeside office that hired out the pleasure boats on the lake. It was a small building, plate glass front window, red front door. Sign writing that displayed its somewhat unoriginal name. "Medina Pleasure Boat Hire".

Brenner walked in. A bell tinkled above the door. A middle age man stood behind the counter. He looked like every man that police witnesses described as, average. Mid-length, medium brown hair. Brown eyes. Oval face. Slightly uneven teeth. Five ten, maybe. Behind him on the wall a plaque. "You don't have to be mad to work here, but it helps".

For a short second Brenner wanted to punch the man. For no reason other than his utter inoffensiveness offended the big man. He was like a void where a person should have been. Taking up oxygen and nutrients from some other person who actually occupied the space they lived in.

But Brenner knew his feelings were both unkind and unfair, so he crushed them down and plastered a huge fake smile on his face to make amends.

It was a terrifying thing to witness, and the inoffensive man shrank back as Brenner approached.

'Howdy, friend,' greeted Brenner. All canines and suppressed anger. 'I believe you are the man who rents out that large paddleboat.'

The man nodded, his face pale as he stared at the six feet five, three-hundred-pound biker that had walked into his shop and exposed his teeth to him.

'I wonder if you could tell me who is currently renting it, and how long they'll be on it. Also, their itinerary if they have one?'

'I'm not at liberty to tell you that,' replied the man, his voice barely above a whisper. Then he shook his head. 'I'm sorry. I don't know why I said that. I'm sure I can make an exception. What can I tell you? And please don't hurt me.'

Brenner raised an eyebrow then glanced at the man's chest. He was wearing a name tag. In an office of one. It read, Benjamin.

'Look, I'm not going to hurt you,' said Brenner, 'Unless, of course, you would like me to hurt you, Benjamin. Would you like me to hurt you, Benjamin?'

Benjamin shook his head.

'Well then don't be stupid,' continued Brenner. 'Now, who is on the boat? Tell all you know.'

'I don't know much,' admitted Benjamin. 'The man that hired the boat was foreign. Arab, I think. But the group seemed mixed. Arabs, Russian, maybe, Croatian. Not sure, but not all the same. About twenty of them.'

'How long they got the boat for?'

'An initial two weeks. With an option to extend.'

'What's their itinerary? Are they going to sail around or just anchor in the middle like they ae now?'

Benjamin shook his head. 'I'm real sorry, I don't know. Usually I would have an idea, because we have our own captain on board as well as a full staff, chef, waiters, maids, and deckhands, but the Arab wanted no strangers on board. He insisted his men could do the job.'

'Is that usual?'

'No,' admitted Benjamin. 'Actually, it's not strictly even legal. But ...'

'He offered you a big stack of money,' said Brenner.

Benjamin nodded. 'More than I usually make in six months.'

The big man looked down at the jetty, perusing the boats lashed up. 'Got any speedboats for hire?'

Benjamin nodded. 'Nothing outrageous. But that red one has a healthy turn of speed. You want it?'

Brenner nodded. 'For later.'

'You got ID?'

Brenner put down a large stack of money.

CHAPTER FORTY-FOUR

The big man had gone through countless different plans. But they were all minor variations on the same theme. Get speedboat. Go to paddleboat. Terminate all with extreme prejudice.

The fact there would be no collateral damage simplified things even further.

So, finally, Brenner decided to simplify to the extreme. A plan that had been boiled down to its most basic parts.

Firstly, he waited until dark. Then he opened the saddlebag on his Harley and extracted the FLASH Dave had given him. The FLame Assault SHoulder Weapon. Designated, M202A1. It's four tubes were loaded with the second batch of 66 mm incendiary rockets and each warhead contained approximately one and a half pounds of napalm.

He carried the weapon down to the quay, climbed into his rented speedboat and cruised slowly out toward the paddleboat. Two hundred yards away he extended the barrel, mounted it on his shoulder, took careful aim and fired.

All four rockets leapt from the launcher at once, racing toward the paddleboat, streaming lines of fire behind them.

The salvo struck the boat directly amidships and broke its back. The two separate pieces burst into violent conflagration and a greasy ball of fire climbed heavenwards like an atomic strike. Even two hundred yards away, Brenner had to turn his head away from the blast to avoid the heat drying out his eyes.

Once he got back to the jetty there was only a small patch of flame left on the water.

Retribution.

The Harley thundered off into the night.

CHAPTER FORTY-FIVE

Brenner stayed under cover all day and now it was ten in the evening and he was scanning the office block in front of him.

Taylor's apartment was on the top floor. It was obvious that, being the boss, he had emptied the office block, ensuring everyone went home at five o'clock.

It was also just as obvious the place was a massive maze of corridors that would contain countless protectors ready to spring a trap. Not least the five men patrolling outside the entrance and the five further men in the lobby.

Once again, the enemy had inadvertently assisted Brenner by ensuring there would be no chance for collateral damage. However, Brenner would bet ten to one there were at least another ten men in the building. Maybe even more. They would be at choke points, or random floors. Tooled up and waiting.

To simply go in through the front door and fight his way to the top was suicide. Too many well-trained men with assault rifles.

He leaned back against a tree and thought, searching for a plan.

After an hour he had very little. And what he did have was merely a slight variation on storming the building like a medieval knight, slashing and killing all who stood before him.

'Oh well,' the big man mumbled to himself as he disrobed, ready to change. 'Needs must, I suppose. It is what it is.'

Then man became Wolfman, and death ran free once again.

The office building was designed with the bottom four floors twenty percent larger than the top floors. This meant the building was like a tall block stacked on top of a squat block. The lower block was criss-crossed with exterior steel frames, like a massive piece of modern art.

The top was as sleek and smooth as a Hollywood facelift. Brenner knew he could easily climb to the outside of the fourth floor, but no higher. There was no purchase on the building above that point.

But it was better than nothing.

He planned to hit the exterior guards first then, while the lobby guards were waiting for him to enter, he would climb to the fourth floor and come at them from inside the building. Hitting them from behind. He only hoped he didn't run into another contingent between the first and fourth floors as he went down, as that would negate his element of surprise.

He had already noted the exterior guards were toting the suppressed version of the Heckler Koch MP5 submachine gun. He assumed this was because, even though Taylor had a lot of political sway, he didn't want the obvious sounds of a full fire fight going down outside his primary residence.

Brenner had no doubt the guns in the interior would be of a heavier caliber and unsilenced.

The exterior group of five men had decided on a static protection setting. Fanned out in a semicircle in front of the front door. Brenner sneaked around to the rear entrance and saw the door had been well booby trapped. Filament thin wires ran from the door to a series of claymores that would shred anything that attempted to enter that way. Obvious, overkill and highly effective.

But that didn't bother him as he wasn't going to try to enter that way. Instead he scaled the wall and, using the hatching of steel bars, he moved quickly around the building at a height of around thirty feet.

Blending with the shadows he edged to the front of the building and, when he was above the group of guards, he simply launched himself off the building.

The one second the guards were nervously scanning the surrounds for an intruder, the next second, hell dropped in to become intimately acquainted.

The men were good. They were veterans of countless battles and skirmishes. They were the product of a well-trained army that had, at one stage, been the most powerful in Africa. And they were fit, fast, and deadly.

Silenced submachine guns purred as they spat out their payloads. FMJ slugs ricocheted and buzzed through the air like spiteful metal wasps. Men grunted in effort as they tried to tag the massive midnight monster that had appeared as if from nowhere.

But the monster was too fast. Too furious. And just too darn bad.

Brenner left the bodies where they lay as he ran and sprung onto the side of the building, climbing up at a speed that would have caused Spiderman to give pause.

Brennerwolf, five - enemy, zero

The first move of a deadly chess game had been taken. Now it was all about massive amounts of speed and aggression.

When he reached the ledge on the fourth floor, the Wolfman gathered himself and looked for a point where he might achieve ingress without attracting too much attention. However, the modern building had no opening windows and the only way in was through one of the floor-to-ceiling panes of strengthened glass.

He bunched his muscles and slammed into one of the panes, smashing through easily but noisily. Without pausing to think he simply ran down the stairs as fast as he could, taking entire landings in a single leap. Ten leaps later he burst through the back door of the lobby and attacked.

The fireteam of five men were all still facing outwards in an attempt to see what had taken down their compatriots. Brenner dispatched two of them before the rest had even had a chance to turn around.

M16 A4s fired in burst mode but Brennerwolf easily evaded them, cutting and slashing as he ducked and rolled.

Seconds later … Brennerwolf, ten - enemy, zero.

He moved on, trusting on shock and awe as he barreled up the stairs at a speed that defied belief, smashing through doors and checking each corridor as he proceeded upward.

On the sixth floor he ran into the next fireteam.

M16s clattered, men screamed. Brennerwolf howled as he took a three-round burst to his left shoulder.

Blood flowed. Men died.

Brennerwolf, fifteen - enemy, zero.

Death moved onwards and upward.

He sensed the next team before he actually broke down the door. Twenty-second floor. He took a deep breath, tensed, then kicked the door as hard as he could, making sure he struck it dead center so it flew off its hinges and whipped down the corridor like a projectile.

And he was right behind it, mauling and biting. A whirlwind of tooth and claw.

A round to the abdomen. Ricochet. A glancing blow but enough to draw blood. Rend flesh.

Brennerwolf, twenty - enemy, zero.

He paused to get his breath then continued upward.

Speed.

Then he was at the top. Outside the door that led to the penthouse. Instead of the usual utilitarian, gray, plain door, this boasted solid oak paneling, a brass handle, and a discreet electronic lock and keypad.

The final play.

CHAPTER FORTY-SIX

Leroux played out the assault in his mind, following the sounds of battle as the assailant got closer. And closer.

Steady, boys he's close,' he instructed his men. 'Karl,' he continued to the man behind the .50 cal machine gun. 'You keep your finger on that trigger. On my command you open fire, right?'

'Right, Boss,' responded the veteran. 'On your command.'

They waited. The only sound, their breathing.

The seconds became minutes. The minutes stretched into infinity.

Leroux was relying on instinct more than the usual senses of sight, sound, and smell. He was accessing a deeper level of awareness. That ancient consciousness that told a man when a sabre tooth tiger was lurking, about to pounce. The tingle on the back of one's neck. The feeling of an unknown presence. It was the level of perception most veterans had. And it was the reason the really good ones survived, while all around them, other men died.

Microseconds before Brennerwolf kicked down the door, Leroux punched the air in command. 'Fire,' he shouted.

Karl depressed the trigger and the M2 spewed out .50 caliber rounds at a rate of four hundred and fifty a minute.

From the moment Brenner came through the doorway to the time he got to the machine gun, just over a half a second elapsed. A slow blink of an eye. But in that microscopic moment of time, Karl had managed to fire exactly four rounds. Three of them struck Brennerwolf.

The massive impacts slowed the four-hundred-pound monster down, but they didn't stop it. Brennerwolf literally tore Karl's head from his shoulders then, holding it in his hand, he used it to smash the remaining two mercenaries to the floor.

That left Leroux.

The Afrikaner pulled out his Colt 45 and emptied the seven-round magazine directly into Brenner's chest at point blank range.

Brenner stumbled slightly then he grabbed Leroux by the face and pummeled him into the wall. The mercenary fought back but Brenner's fading strength was still too much to handle and, seconds later, there was an audible crack and Leroux's lifeless body slumped to the floor, his neck a mere collection of shattered bone.

Brennerwolf fell to his knees, blood pouring from his wounds. Two of the .50 cal rounds had struck him in his stomach and the third, high up on his chest. And although his body was trying to heal, the wounds were simply too massive.

Gathering the last remnants of his strength, Brenner stood and charged the final door, breaking it off its hinges as he barreled through.

Brandon Taylor was waiting for him. Standing in the entrance area. In his right hand a Smith and Wesson .44 magnum. His hand was shaking, his eyes wild with panic and fear.

Brennerwolf threw back his head and howled.

Taylor dropped his weapon and fell to the floor, covering his ears with his hands, like a child trying to block out the cries of the bogeyman.

The Wolfman limped over to the oilman, grabbed him by his hair and lifted him up, holding him at eye level, his feet some six inches from the floor.

'Guilty,' rumbled Brennerwolf.

'Please,' whimpered the oilman.

The Wolfman shook his head. 'No.'

And, with all his remaining strength he threw Taylor against the opposite wall. The body struck with the same sound as a melon being dropped from a high place onto the sidewalk.

Brennerwolf turned slowly and limped to the elevators, each step coming slower and more painfully than the last. His breath came in ragged gasps and his vision blurred from grays to black.

When the elevator arrived, Brennerwolf stared at the buttons for a full minute before he worked out which one to push.

On the interminable journey down, he passed out twice.

His Harley was only a block away. But Brenner knew with almost complete certainty he wasn't going to make it.

Brennerwolf, twenty-five. Enemy … one?

CHAPTER FORTY-SEVEN

The door to the lobby opened automatically, allowing Brennerwolf to crawl through.

He managed to get twenty yards outside the building then his body shut down. He simply wasn't healing fast enough; he had lost too much blood and the massive shock imparted from the three .50 cal rounds had shattered bone and smashed vital organs.

It was over.

So, it was with a feeling of relief he allowed himself to stop trying and just lay down on the sidewalk and let the darkness take him. No more pain. No more fighting other people's wars. No more life-and-death decisions.

No more.

But he couldn't slip away. He felt himself being rolled over onto his back. Then someone slapped his face. Hard.

He opened his eyes and struggled to focus. Light. Dark. A face. Smiling. Unusual teeth.

'No, no, no,' said Solomon. 'I didn't follow you all this way to have you die on me. No fucking way. Lenny, sit him up.'

Brennerwolf felt someone grab him under his shoulders and pull him to a seating position.

Solomon slapped him again, rocking his head to the side. 'Wakey, wakey, big boy,' he said. 'Uncle

Solomon is here to make things better. Then it's time to return to the Project.'

Brenner shook his head. 'No,' he mumbled. 'Can't go back. Leave me.'

'Sorry, my friend,' answered Solomon. 'No can do.' As he spoke, he took a syringe full of a red liquid from his coat pocket and removed the plastic safety cap. 'I'm going to give you a shot of the serum,' said the man in black. 'It's what keeps me in such fine fettle. Now, it is going to hurt like bejesus. But it will enhance your healing. Get you back on your feet. Probably be some serious side effects, but the colonel can deal with those at the Project.'

Brennerwolf batted ineffectually at the syringe. Too weak to stop Solomon. 'No, please,' he mumbled. 'No more injections. No more experiments. No more running. Just let me die.'

Solomon jabbed the needle into the Wolfman's neck and pressed the plunger.

Brenner felt like liquid fire had been injected directly into his veins. The level of pain was indescribable. For a brief moment, he wondered if Solomon felt this every time he injected himself. To go through this twice a day was purgatory in the extreme.

But as the pain scoured his body, he started to feel his flesh knitting back together. Nothing miraculous, but instead of being at death's door, he at least felt like he was a few paces away.

He tried to stand, bracing his body so he could fight back. But Lenny held him in a grip of steel, his strength an unsurmountable mountain.

Solomon gestured at Lenny. 'Come on. Pick him up, it's time he came home.'

Brenner struggled as hard as he could. Throwing his head back in an attempt to butt Lenny in the face. Kicking and thrashing about. Snarling and biting. 'No,' he shouted. 'You have no right. No right to take my freedom. To lock me up, experiment on me.'

'You signed up for it,' answered Solomon. 'We all knew what we were getting into.'

'Fuck you,' yelled Brennerwolf, his voice a guttural growl. 'I never signed up for anything. I woke up in a laboratory and that was that. Next thing I was a fucking Wolfman. You son of a bitch.'

Solomon scowled. That wasn't right. He had volunteered with alacrity, proud to serve his country in any way possible.

But then he remembered what Matty had told him about Lenny. Taken as a child. Held against his will. And a momentary flicker of doubt crossed his mind. But he crushed it down. The colonel must have his reasons. Whatever he did was for the good of the country. The good of America, the land of the free. Sometimes sacrifices had to be made.

He shook his head. 'Sorry, big man. Orders are orders. Come on Lenny, let's go.' He turned and started to walk back to the limousine that Howard was waiting in. Parked two blocks away.

But Lenny didn't follow. Instead, he helped Brenner to his feet and steadied him. Leaving him to stand alone.

Then he gave him a slight push in the opposite direction that Solomon was walking. 'Go,' he said.

Brennerwolf's face registered his surprise, but he didn't stop to question the gesture.

Slowly, with dragging feet, he started to walk away.

'Hey,' Solomon shouted at Lenny. 'What the hell do you think you're doing?'

'Letting him go,' said the man mountain.

Solomon shook his head. 'Afraid not, headache boy. No such luck.'

And the man in black moved to intercept the Wolfman. But as he did so, Lenny burst into motion, slamming into Solomon like a Mack truck, hammering him to the ground with a sickening crunch of breaking bones and tearing flesh. Solomon fought back, his flesh healing at its usual phenomenal rate. But Lenny was all over him, like ugly on a moose. Fists, elbows, head. Striking hard and fast, bringing his superior strength into play, breaking and re-breaking limbs as he did so.

Solomon clawed and bit and struck back. But it was like punching a giant Redwood tree. A pointless task.

Lenny bled from a hundred rips and tears in his flesh, but he ignored the pain and simply concentrated on keeping Solomon down.

Then Brennerwolf was gone. Disappearing into the night. Seconds later the growl of a Harley could be heard fading into the distance.

Both Solomon and Lenny stopped fighting.

Neither spoke for a while.

Solomon simply stood still and stared at the man mountain.

Lenny also stood, but he clutched at his head as he did so. Moaning softly at the internal pain that far exceeded the multitude of deep wounds that covered the rest of his body.

Finally, Solomon asked. 'Why?'

Lenny looked up. 'I saw his wings,' he said. 'Stretched out above him. They were so beautiful. I never knew he had them before. Big black wings.'

'Don't be stupid,' snapped Solomon. But he shivered as he retaliated. Because he had seen something. Not wings as such. But something suggestive of them. A huge lurking shadow that loomed over Brenner for a moment. Then it was gone. He had found no beauty in the vision.

Lenny sat; his legs splayed out in front of him like a child in a sandpit. He still clutched his head in his hands. Then, as slow as a falling tree, he collapsed sideways and lay still.

Solomon knelt beside him. 'Hey, big boy,' he said. 'Come on, pull yourself together. Let's get you back to the project. The colonel will fix you. Okay?'

Lenny shook his head. 'No fixing Lenny,' he whispered. 'I can't hardly breathe.'

Solomon stroked the hair from the man mountain's eyes. 'Get up. Come on, you can do it.'

'My head isn't sore anymore.'

'See, that's a good sign,' urged Solomon. 'You're getting better.'

Lenny smiled.

And died.

CHAPTER FORTY-EIGHT

Solomon stood at perfect attention, eyes forward, heels together, toes slightly apart, thumb parallel with his trouser seams. There was time for insouciance and times for strict military protocol.

This was the time for stringent adherence to procedure.

'So, you lost him,' stated the colonel.

'Sir.'

'Again.'

'Yes, sir,' agreed Solomon.

'And you lost PFC Lenny Kozlowski.'

'Sir,' replied Solomon. 'Strictly speaking, PFC Kozlowski died. Some sort of tumor.'

'On your watch, Sergeant.'

'Yes, sir.'

The colonel rose from his leather chair and walked over to the window. The blinds were closed. With a twist of his wrist, he tweaked them open. Slightly. A sliver of yellow sunlight knifed across the room to rest on Solomon's shoes. The man in black flinched but did not move.

Slowly, the colonel continued twisting the cord. The sliver of sunlight traveled up Solomon's legs, crept across his chest and stopped just before it reached his exposed neck.

Neither man spoke for a while. Solomon stood at attention and the colonel gazed out of the window.

After almost three minutes the colonel spoke. 'We need Brenner.'

'Yes, sir.'

'No, Solomon. You don't seem to understand. We. Need. Brenner. Without him, Project Bloodborn is at risk. Everything we have worked for over the last fifty years could very well come to nothing. It all relies on having access to the Wolfman.'

'Permission to speak freely, sir.'

The colonel nodded.

'Surely you exaggerate, sir,' said Solomon. 'After all, we have many successful candidates that have come out of the Project. Granted, there have been some flaws, but on the whole, you have created men that are superhuman. Soldiers that are far superior to the standard grunt in the field, sir. Perhaps we are putting too much emphasis on Brenner. After all, he is but one man.'

The colonel spun on his heel and walked up to Solomon, stopping only when his face was uncomfortably close. Noses almost touching. 'Idiot,' he said.

Solomon balked at the insult.

'You compare our other results to Sergeant Brenner? What results? Lenny Kozlowski? With his barely useable IQ and a tumor the size of a grapefruit in his head. The countless other freaks we have produced that are riddled with cancers, or congenital defects. Or worse, simply insane. Yourself? You cannot go out in the daylight. You need a constant supply of the serum to stay alive. Could we drop you into enemy territory and let you fend for yourself?

No. Never. You can't even carry enough serum with you to last more than a week. Useless.

'But Brenner, he can survive off the land. Fend for himself. He needs no weapons, no resupplies, no backup. He is the only shifter we have created that can change at will. Imagine ten of him. Or a hundred. Dropped behind enemy lines. There would be no stopping them.'

'But, sir,' insisted Solomon. 'Surely we have tried to recreate Brenner? We must have all the relevant information.'

The colonel nodded. 'Of course, we have tried. A hundred times. Two hundred. Not one candidate has lived through the process. There is something about Brenner. Something special. Yet another reason we need him, Sergeant. Desperately need him.'

'I understand, sir.'

'Good. Now go to the quartermaster, draw enough serum for two weeks. Then go and find Brenner. And do not fail me again, Sergeant Hopewell. Your continued existence depends upon it.'

Solomon saluted, about turned and marched from the room.

The colonel took out his hand sanitizer, pumped a dollop onto his hands and worked it in, rubbing hard. Again. And again.

And over six hundred miles away, a big man on a black Harley Davidson rat bike, thundered north.

A knight on a dark horse. His personal code of honor his only armor. His body his only weapon.

And behold, the third horseman rode a black horse. And in his hands, he carried the scales of justice.

*And I thought that I heard a voice decry ... I am Venge-
ance.*

FINI

Well, there you go. Ded lives. Hooray!

If you enjoyed this – here is a sample of the next in
the series – WOLF WARRIOR…

CHAPTER ONE – Wolf Warrior

Brenner was in Montana, a few miles from the Canadian border. He had contacted Griff two weeks before, telling him he needed some time alone. Then he had left San Antonio and taken a random and varied route through Arkansas, Missouri, Iowa, and South Dakota. Taking it easy. Riding slow and stopping often to eat and rest.

Healing.

He had suffered through the full moon in Missouri.

The 'Show Me' state.

Show me a werewolf.

Physically, Brenner had fully healed. Mentally … not so much.

When he had been travelling through the backroads of Iowa he had stopped for a rest and spotted a herd of Whitetail deer. Fifteen in all. Three bucks, eight does. And four fawns, small and dappled and still unsteady on their tiny hooves.

As he had seen them he had been instantly overcome with an all-consuming killing rage and had exploded into full wolf mode. Mere minutes later he had reverted back to his human form, covered in blood, and surrounded by the ragged and dismembered remains of the herd. Even the fawns. Torn to shreds in a frenzy of killing. Killing for no reason other than a black and unstoppable rage.

A few days later, riding on a trail through South Dakota, he had come across a river barring his way. A small tributary that flowed into the larger Missouri. There were remnants of a wooden bridge, four posts and a scattering of planks. Rather than search for another place to cross he had decided to simply ford across instead.

The plan was simple, morph into Wolfman mode, carry the Harley across to the other side, continue journey.

But the moment Brenner had become the Wolfman, the world changed. A tsunami of rage crashed over him. Engulfing him in a dark sea of hatred and fury. His vision went red and the urge to kill eliminated every other emotion.

His senses went into hyperdrive. Sight, hearing, smell. He could sense people. Far away. Perhaps ten miles or so. Their life-light a beacon to his newfound rage. And the wolf inside him howled and roared for their demise. *They Are Weak*, it screamed.

Kill Them.

Destroy Them All.

But the tiny part of him that was still Brenner fought back. Refusing to kill for no reason. Denying the monster inside.

And with the greatest of willpower, he changed back into human form.

Then he simply lay on the ground, exhausted. His breath coming in heaving gasps. His head pounding, his muscles shuddering and twitching from the surfeit of adrenaline that had pumped through him.

'The serum,' he said to himself. It had cured his wounds, but it was not designed for him. It was tailor made for Solomon and his particular genetic makeup. With Brenner it had ramped his aggression up to un-manageable levels.

If he changed, he would kill. And he would con-tinue to kill, until someone or something stopped him. And worse, Brenner knew the serum was not a run of the mill drug. It was not something that would simply wear off, given time. No. It was a genomic modifier. It had affected Brenner at a DNA level.

And its effects would be permanent.

His healing, speed, and strength would remain, but Ded Brenner knew one thing for certain … he could no longer risk changing into either his Wolf or his Wolf-man form ever again. The risk of massive collateral damage would be far too great.

His curse was now truly a curse in both name and nature.

He was a ravening wolf trapped inside a man's body.

A beast.

And he could never be let free.

So, with a heavy heart, he rode on, heading for Montana and the Canadian border. Heading for the wilderness.

To be alone.

Or as close to alone as possible in the modern world.

The colonel seldom left his rooms anymore. An office, bedroom, bathroom, and a small gymnasium. In fact, he had seldom left the compound in which Project Bloodborn was situated for over twenty years. A virtual hermit. An obsessive recluse bent on achieving his goal above all else.

The creation of a controllable super-soldier that would raise America's combat capabilities to a level never achievable by the enemy.

And by the enemy, the colonel meant, everybody else on the planet who was not American.

Apart from Sergeant Ded Brenner, the Project had not achieved his goal.

They had come close on many occasions. Subjects like Sergeant Solomon Hopewell, flawed by his inability to operate in the sunlight, and his absolute reliance on tri-daily doses of the serum.

Or PFC Lenny Kozlowski. As strong as a main battle tank but with a child's IQ and perception, and a tumor the size of a grapefruit in his skull.

Or countless other almost-rans. All falling at the final hurdle due to some fault or other. Cancers, faulty genetics, random diseases, or catastrophic spontaneous genetic unravelling.

Not like Brenner. Self-contained. Deadly. Operating completely autonomously and utterly unstoppable. If they could reproduce the Wolfman in a slightly more compliant host then they would have the ultimate soldier.

The ultimate weapon of mass destruction.

Then the world would know what it was to be American. Because with a thousand like Brenner, the red, white, and blue would fly proudly over the soil of every nation on earth.

All would sing the same national anthem.

Proudly American.

And now, for the first time, it looked as though the laboratory had come up with a viable alternative.

The doctor stood opposite the colonel, his laptop on the desk, a slight smile on his face. His excitement palpable.

'You say that the subjects are stable?' asked the colonel.

Doctor Mengele nodded his affirmation. Close cropped iron gray hair, dark eyes crowned by black, bushy eyebrows. Slightly misaligned teeth and a non-existent top lip.

He looked to be a fit man in his late fifties, perhaps early sixties. He was actually one hundred and six years old, exceeding the colonel's age by two whole years. A definite perk of working for The Project and its rafts of genomic and genetic research. Although they had not yet stumbled across the fountain of youth, as such, they had most definitely discovered the fountain of eternal middle-age.

'How many survived the seasoning?' continued the colonel.

At this question, Doctor Mengele's smile dropped. 'You must understand, Colonel,' he prevaricated. 'The process of adaption is an extremely rigorous one, after all, we are changing human beings into an entirely different genus. From *Homo Sapiens* to an amorphous blend of *Homo* and *Hyaenidae*. We have called it, *Hyaenidae Sapiens*.'

'How many?' repeated the colonel.

'Well, of the initial sixty-four, umm … volunteers, seven have survived. Of those, three have achieved the ability to shape shift at will, although they are unstable and sometimes shift without meaning to. Sometimes to half-human mode, and other times to full beast mode. The other four are more of a permanent hybrid, the *Hyaenidae* having dominated the *Homo Sapiens* side on a permanent basis.'

'Explain,' commanded the colonel.

Mengele leaned forward and tapped his laptop, bringing the screen to life. Then he turned it to face the colonel. 'Here, it is easier to show than to tell.'

A handheld camera. The sound hollow, full of white noise. A row of cages. Each one separated from the next by three feet of empty space. The bars at least two inches thick. The doors locked with three solid steel bars and padlocked hinges. Impenetrable.

Stark electric bulbs hung from the ceiling. Concrete floor. In each cell a single steel bed with a blanket and a thin cotton mattress. Chemical toilet. A large bowl of drinking water. The cells are clearly marked from one to seven.

'Cell number one contains the Alpha,' explained Mengele. 'The strongest, and the one who is in most control of his metamorphic capabilities. We have called him Anubis. The other two shapeshifters are Osiris and Set. The four permanent hybrids are simply referred to as H-one, H-two, H-three and H-four.'

The colonel studied the screen. Cell one contained a predominantly humanoid subject. Six feet, maybe two hundred pounds. He was naked, and his musculature stood out to the point it looked somehow false. Like someone had created a rough facsimile of the human body using raw concrete. Slabs and hunks of striated muscle with little grace or form.

'Why is he standing like that?' asked the colonel. 'All hunched over. Does he have a hunchback?'

'Strictly speaking, no,' answered doctor Mengele. 'A hunched back, or Kyphosis, is an abnormality of the spine. What you are seeing is muscular. You see, one of the reasons we chose the Hyena as the primary donor is its bite is amongst the most powerful in the world. Stronger than either a lion or even a grizzly bear. And one of the main reasons for this is the huge band of muscle running from the top of the head, down the back. These are, ostensibly, the creatures jaw muscles. We retained that as one of its primary weapons. Hence, the hump of muscle.'

The colonel nodded. 'Not a problem. They haven't been bred for looks. As long as they can pass for human, I'm satisfied. How long until we can field test them?'

'A week,' answered the doctor. 'Maybe two. A couple of small problems with discipline we need to iron out, then we'll be good to go.'

'Well that is excellent news,' said the colonel. 'That is excellent news indeed.'

✳✳✳

Thanks again for reading. If you would like to get in touch, my email is

zuffs@sky.com

Give me a shout if you got something to talk about.

Bye for now – your friend in words

Craig